Scent of a White Rose

Book one of The Rose Trilogy

Tish Thawer

Sabrina,
Enjoy the roses,
but beware of the
thorns!
Happy Reading

Tish
Thawer

Scent of a White Rose

by

Tish Thawer

Amber Leaf Publishing

Divide, Colorado

First Edition
First Printing, 2011
ISBN: 978-0-9849886-1-7

Library of Congress Control Number: 2011963550

Cover design by Regina Wamba of Mae I Design and Photography
Free stock photo of woman courtesy of Marcus Ranum /ranum.com
Edited by Kara Malinczak

Amber Leaf Publishing, Divide, Colorado
www.tishthawer.com

ACKNOWLEDGMENTS

Many thanks to my family for putting up with me while I was immersed in Rose and Christian's story. The missed dinners, the odd writing hours, the annoying questions I would randomly throw your direction...thank you for all of your support and, I love you guys with all my heart.

Special thanks go to my wonderful husband, Dee. You were more than a sounding board, but a true contributor to the direction in which The Rose Trilogy ended up heading. I love you more than you'll ever know.

To my mom and dad, who have not only encouraged me in everything that I've ever done in my life, but who kept on my butt, asking me every day, "Is your book done yet?", in an effort to show their excitement and belief in this project. I love you both. Mom, a special thanks for instilling the love of books in me, even if it did take 30+ years, and for your eagle eye.

To my amazing cover artist and friend, Regina Rasmussen

Wamba. You took an idea and turned it into magic. Thank you for putting up with my perfectionism and control issues. (Yes, I admit it—I'm a control freak!)

To my wonderful editor Kara Malinczak, thank you for all your hard work to make this something that we could both be proud of. You rock my socks off!!

To Kiersten Fay, thank you for answering all the random questions that I sent your way. You are a guiding light.

To Desirae Hennington, your insight and passion truly helped lead me in the right direction. Thank you.

And to Caris Roane—A special thanks for your willingness to take me under your wing and for all of your amazing guidance, but mostly, for your friendship. You are an inspiration.

* * * * *

Rose's eye blinks, an idea blooms,

But who could've imagined the impending doom?

* * * * *

CHAPTER ONE

Wide Awake

(Rose)

I opened my eyes and felt death. The presence of it, the weight of it, the sadness of it. I couldn't believe my mom was gone. I thought *the weight of it* described it best. It felt like a weight on my chest...one that would never get lighter.

Dad said that we'd be okay. "Time heals everything, Rose," he always told me in that solemn tone of voice. I didn't believe him. How could I, when I could tell that he didn't even believe it?

But honestly, I didn't want time to pass. I just wanted to lay here on my bed, wide awake in my black funeral clothes, and stare at the ceiling. I just wanted to lay here remembering when my mom and I had painted my room and hung those stars and moons. They weren't the stick-on, glow-in-the-dark kind. They were beautiful crystals in all sizes and colors strung from my freshly painted black ceiling. They danced and gleamed just like we had imagined. Well, just like she had imagined. It had been her idea...my mom, the crafty one.

With a spark of wonder in her voice she'd said, "It will be beautiful and you'll feel like you're sleeping under the twinkling stars every night." I wasn't convinced. But when we were done, we opened the curtains to let the moonlight flow in, and I was speechless. She'd been right. I'd been amazed as I watched the beautiful little stars and moons twinkle and spin right there in my very own room. God, I love my mom.

I didn't want time to pass. I wanted it to reverse.

* * * * *

(Rose)

My mom, Loraine Reynolds, was killed in a "freak

accident." Someone broke into our house in the dead of night,

and when they found my mom coming out of her room, they

killed her.

That doesn't sound too freaky, right? Your average burglary

gone wrong. I guess what made it "freaky," was that the cops

were baffled by *how* she had been killed.

The only evidence of violence was two small puncture

wounds on her neck. At first they thought she'd been stabbed by

an ice pick or something, which was strange enough, but then

came the *really* strange part. Her body had been drained of all the

blood. See…*freaky*, right?

The robbers didn't take anything. The cops assumed that

they must have panicked and left in a hurry. There were no fingerprints or DNA left at the scene, and no trail for them to follow. After receiving nothing but countless apologies, we faced the fact that we were never going to get an explanation as to how or why my mom had been killed.

It's now been about six months since the accident. My dad has gone back to work and I've gone back to school. My college is only about twenty minutes away, but you'd think it was in a third-world country from the way my dad has been treating me. I understand that he's freaked. And, I understand that I'm now the only family he has left, which he reminds me of on a daily basis. But damn it, I'm twenty years old, and I'm not a child.

But, every time I look at him, and I see the sadness in his eyes, and watch the emotions roll across his face, I hold my tongue. Because he's right; I am the only family he has left. So, if he wants to treat me like I'm ten instead of twenty, that's okay. If he wants to have one of his company cars take me and pick me up from school, that's okay. And if he insists that I live with him until I graduate college, that's okay. But I'll be damned if he's going to stop me from seeing Christian.

CHAPTER TWO

White Rose

(Rose)

"Dad, I just want to go have dinner with some of my friends after school. Why is that such a big deal?" My voice rang with exasperation.

"Why is that such a big deal? Really, Rose? You have to ask that?" He was clearly just as frustrated as I was. "It's a big deal because this is a dangerous world and you of all people should understand that. I'm sorry, but I just don't like the idea of you being out after dark."

I tried to smooth my voice into one of an adult filled with compassion. "Dad, it's been six months. I miss Mom too, and I will *never* forget what happened to her. But we can't live our lives in fear."

"I'm not living in fear; I'm living in reality. I lost my wife, and I refuse to lose my daughter to the evil of this world, too." He sounded defeated as he scooted his chair away from the table.

I knew this was how the conversation would go, but you can't blame a girl for trying. I really wish he would've said yes, because I'm sick of lying and sneaking around. But what am I supposed to do? I can't just let him drag me down. I want to go on with my life...it's what my mom would have wanted.

As I watched my father put his breakfast dish in the sink, place both hands on the counter and hang his head, I knew I couldn't fight him on this. Just like always...Dad wins.

Resolved to be the innocent "white Rose" he pictured me to be, I said, "Okay Dad. I'll be home before sunset. Do you want me to pick something up for dinner or do you want to do it?"

"Actually, I have a dinner meeting that I have to attend, so just have the driver stop somewhere and get yourself some takeout. And no calling for delivery. I will not have strangers coming to this house, even if it is just to deliver food."

I started to protest. I was frustrated that he could totally dismiss my plans and insist that I come straight home after school when he wasn't even going to be there. But then, it dawned on me...this was the perfect opportunity. It looked like I'd be skipping dinner with my friends and opting for a little road trip instead.

"Okay. I'll just grab something then, but what time should I expect you home?" I asked innocently.

"Probably around 9 p.m." He spun around, straightened his shoulders, and plastered a loving smile on his face. "I love you, Rose. Thanks for humoring an old man who cares too much."

Well, now I just felt like crap. "You're welcome Dad. I love you too."

As I listened to the front door close, I looked down into the sink and watched our breakfast slide down the drain. White, runny eggs swirling their way down into the dark hole towards the disposal. That was me…a white substance, fading and running like watercolors down a drain into the dark. Man, I wished I didn't have to lie to him.

As I climbed into the shower, I realized that not only did I have to figure out how I was going to ditch my driver today, but also how I was going to get a hold of Christian to let him know I was coming down. He always said, "Don't try to reach me before dark. I'm dead to the world."

I knew he slept for most of the day because of his job, but man, it made trying to plan a spontaneous rendezvous a little tricky. Well, that was just it! I wouldn't tell him I was coming down. I'd surprise him.

Christian worked at a nightclub on the outskirts of town. I'd been there plenty of times, but had never gone in. Not for the obvious reason that I was only twenty, but instead because I was usually occupied with Christian lips, as all of my visits revolved around us making out in his car during his breaks. I remembered the first time I saw him. That was a night I'd never forget.

My dad had arranged for my friends and I to be driven in one of his company limos to a concert in Masen, the big city that's about two hours away. We didn't have a curfew, but we were expected to stay with the staff that came with the car. I saw it for the compromise it was; he was letting me go, but with supervision. I guess he'd always been protective, even before Mom's death.

After the concert, we were driving back into town when Jillian loudly announced that she had to use the restroom. The only place around was the nightclub just up the road. It was called "The Rising Pit." I think it had some sort of dance floor in the middle that went up and down using hydraulics. I had never been there, but a few friends of mine had gone and said it was very cool.

Once we reached the nightclub, Jill bounced out of the limo, accompanied by one of the "car crew" as we had taken to calling them, thanked the driver for stopping, and proceeded to make a beeline to the club's front door.

Jill disappeared behind the door, and as I watched it swing shut, a man stepped outside carrying a girl in his arms. I watched from the car as he placed her on her feet, steadying her before letting go. I could tell that she was crying. He was talking to her in what looked like a very gentle manner. She rubbed the tears from her cheeks and then she nodded her head in a "yes" motion. The guy smiled, and I thought I was going to die.

Right then the clouds broke, and he looked like an angel bathed in moonlight. He was so gorgeous. He had to be about 6' 2", and solid muscle from the looks of him. Not bulky like those beefed-up body builders, but very athletic. Wide shoulders, broad chest, thin waist, and what I was sure would be strong, muscled legs. With the moonlight shining on him, I could see he had dark blonde hair with golden highlights, cut short and sharp. I hadn't realized that I was half hanging out the open window of the limo, when he suddenly turned and looked right at me. My breath caught, and I thought I would die…again!

His eyes were so beautiful and so mesmerizing. The intensity of his gaze was piercing. They were an amber color, a rich brown with golden highlights, mixing together like swirled caramel and honey. He was easily the most beautiful thing I'd ever seen.

Right then Jill came barreling out of the nightclub with her escort closely in tow. She was saying something like, "I only wanted a quick shot," and the rest of us started laughing from the car. As she started to walk past the beautiful man, he reached out and tapped her gently on the shoulder. She stopped and he started speaking to her. She kept glancing at the car and then back to him with a huge smile on her face. After a brief moment, he handed her something, then disappeared back inside.

I was so anxious to see what this impossibly gorgeous guy had said to my friend. I was sure it had to do with her only using the facilities instead of being a paying customer or something along those lines, as it was obvious that he worked there.

When Jill got in the car, she sat there for a moment with a "cat-ate-the-mouse" grin on her face. Then she handed me a business card. It was shiny and smooth and had the nightclub's logo on the front. I turned it over and found a hand scribbled note that read, "Roses are red, but I'll be blue, if I'm denied the pleasure, of meeting you. ~ Christian."

My jaw dropped. Jillian was still smiling at me as my other friends started to pass the card back and forth.

Jill proceeded to tell me that he had asked her my name and then scratched out that poem so fast that she could barely see his hand move. He had also included his phone number on the back, and asked that I call him after sunset in two days, which of course, I did.

I started seeing Christian every week, visiting during his breaks and getting seriously serious within those first three months. But then Mom died and everything changed.

My dad, Jeremy Reynolds, is the Vice President of a marketing company here in town, but all his best clients came from the big city. He has to take an overnight business trip once a month to schmooze his big city clients and this is now the only time I get to see Christian. Dad has me stay overnight at Jillian's house whenever he leaves town. So with Jill's help, once a month I lose all sense of morality and sneak out to see my boyfriend. Yeah…it sucks.

* * * * *

CHAPTER THREE

Deviant

(Rose)

After I focused my attention long enough to actually get

dressed, I came up with a plan to ditch the driver/babysitter

after school. It would take some bad behavior on my part, and

then some sweet talk immediately after, but I thought I could

pull it off.

At school I was your average college student. Never stood

out much, kept my nose in the books, and made pretty good

grades. But not today. I was completely disruptive, chatting

when I shouldn't be and constantly dropping stuff and

apologizing loudly. And I was smacking my gum so much that it was actually starting to hurt my jaw.

Finally, I got what I wanted. Mr. Thompson looked up with an exasperated look on his face and said, "Rose Reynolds...see me at the end of the day." *YES!!*

I felt like a deviant over making this much trouble for one of the few teachers that I actually liked. But I knew that Mr. Thompson's only pet peeve was a student who disrupted his lectures, and that is exactly what I'd just done to perfection.

Immediately after my last class, I made my way back up to the 3rd floor to Mr. Thompson's classroom. He was waiting for me at his desk, nose buried in his day planner. "Ms. Reynolds." He acknowledged my presence with a kind, but semi-frustrated tone. "I was not pleased with the way you were constantly interrupting my class today. Is there an explanation that you can give that will keep me from tacking on an additional 500 words to your thesis?"

As I sat down, I tried to make myself look a little shaky.

"I'm so sorry, Mr. Thompson. I think it had something to do with my low-blood sugar. It doesn't happen too often anymore, but after my mom's accident, sometimes I would just forget to eat and then I would end up all shaky and hyper. I'm really sorry." Sincerity was dripping from every word.

Did I say deviant before? I meant criminal. I had actually played the "My mom was killed card" with my history professor just so that I could go make out with a guy.

After Mr. Thompson dismissed me with a sympathetic look and a feather-light warning, I made my way to the first girl's bathroom I could find. I freshened up my makeup and changed my jeans and t-shirt out for the dark blue sundress I had stuffed in my bag. The black flats I had on were going to have to do. Since I was taller than average at 5'10", I didn't wear heels very often anyway. Looking in the mirror, I thought I looked pretty good. The sundress hugged my curves just right, and I certainly had plenty of curves for it to hug. My light blonde hair hung just past my shoulders. I wore it straight most of the time, but today I had braided it for school. So now when I shook it out it was nice and wavy. I loved that trick.

Taking one last glance in the mirror, I applied a final dab to my cherry flavored lipstick. "Time to go see my man!" *Yep, I was giddy!*

As usual, I had arranged to borrow Jill's car for my trip to see Christian. She's such a good friend. She completely feels for me and the strict rules I have to live by. So whenever I can squeeze out from under my dad's thumb, she's totally supportive. *Huh…not sure if that makes her a good friend or a bad one.*

After I parked next to Christian's car, a '67 Mercury Comet Caliente (Yes, it lives up to its name –it is a HOT car!), I checked my lipstick one last time before embarking on the search for my man.

I opened the club's front door and it took my eyes and ears a minute to adjust. The lighting was dark and seductive, and the only sound present was a slow mechanical grinding.

As I looked around, I noticed that I was alone on the main floor. Then I pinpointed the source of the noise. The stage in the middle of the room was moving. I couldn't tell if it was going up or down, and honestly, that was of no interest to me. Instead, I was completely focused on all of the people coming out from underneath it.

I could barely make out the circular staircase that ran around the inside wall underneath the stage, but that's where everyone that I recognized as The Rising Pit's staff was coming from: Bobby, the sexy, blonde DJ; Tori and Dominique, the adorable, redheaded bartenders who were sisters; the gorgeous owner, Evangeline; her muscular, right-hand man and bar manager, Dax; and Christian, head of security, and my boyfriend.

They were all talking and joking, looking more like family than coworkers. Finally the stage had rose all the way up and locked into place with a loud bang, sending shock waves up my legs. Startled, I sucked in a quick breath.

Everyone at the exact same instant snapped their heads in my direction. There was no point in acting shy. They all knew I was Christian's girlfriend. So I cleared my throat, cocked my hip, and gave a little wave directed just at him.

Christian looked surprised, happy, and wary, all at the same time. Once everyone got over their initial shock of seeing me, they dispersed, leaving only Christian and Evangeline to stare in my direction. Before moving off, Evangeline whispered something in Christian's ear. He still had his eyes pinned on mine and a sexy smile on his face, so I figured whatever she had to say to him couldn't be all that bad. I certainly didn't want to get him in trouble for showing up unannounced, but come on, it's a nightclub…party central, and the front door *had* been open.

Evangeline headed towards the back of the club where I assumed her office was. Christian stood there for a moment longer, not moving a muscle, and looking like a Greek God. He was eyeing me up and down, admiring my dress I guess. His sexy smile just kept growing, so I hoped that was an indication that he liked what he saw.

He finally made his way over to me and wrapped me in his arms. "Wow, this is an amazing surprise!" he whispered in my ear as he pulled me close, nuzzling my neck at the same time.

"Yeah, I escaped and thought I'd ditch my friends and come see you instead. This once-a-month shit is for the birds," I said in a husky voice and reached around and grabbed his butt.

Christian and I had made out enough that we were comfortable touching each other, but I needed to let him know it was okay if we took things all the way. As a matter of fact, I was aching for it. It's not like I was a twenty year old virgin for Christ's sake.

He jumped a little as I squeezed his perfect ass with my hand, then looked around to see if anyone was watching…and they were.

He promptly grabbed my hand, flipped off Bobby and Dax, and pulled me out the front door back into the night.

"I'm really glad you came, but you should have called. We're not allowed to have guests here until after 8 p.m. when the club opens," he said as we walked to the corner of the parking lot.

"I thought the club was open. The front door was unlocked and the outside lights were on." I was feeling rather defensive.

Right then, Terrance, one of Christian's security staff, stepped out of the woods just a couple of cars down from where we stood. Christian's eyes narrowed on him, and I could tell by the tension suddenly radiating from his body that he was pissed.

"Terrance, is there a reason why you're out here and the club's standing wide open?"

Terrance looked flushed, but all he said was, "Sorry, boss. I forgot something in my car."

I don't think Christian bought it, and I sure didn't. He hadn't been in the parking lot when I pulled up.

"We'll talk about this later," Christian said. Terrance gave him a clipped nod and headed inside.

"Maybe he was making out with his girlfriend in the woods," I teased, trying to lighten the mood and steer his attention back to the "making out" part of my plans. It must have worked, because in the blink of an eye Christian's hands were all over my body, and his mouth crushed against mine, our tongues fighting for dominance. It was amazing.

"Wow, I guess you really like this dress," I panted between kisses.

"I love your dress, but I'd love it more if it was on the ground," he growled.

His voice was lower than I'd ever heard before, and there was an urgency in the way he kissed me. He grabbed the hem of my dress, raising it slowly as he kissed, sucked and licked at my neck.

This is definitely what I wanted tonight…but outside,

against my friend's car wasn't exactly the sensual fantasy I had envisioned.

Right as Christian settled himself between my legs and started reaching for his belt, the club's front door slammed open. I turned my head to find Evangeline staring right at us. "Christian," she snapped, "I'm sorry to interrupt, but we need to finish opening."

Christian's hands went still, and he slowly raised his head from the side of my neck. He had the most serious look on his face and even though it was dark outside, in that moment, it seemed like *he* was darker too. His eyes were smoky and, they had lost their honey swirl. Even his hair seemed darker, like the highlights had completely disappeared. Suddenly, I wasn't too upset that Evangeline had interrupted.

Christian quickly shook his head and kissed me one last time. He was himself again. "Sorry babe. I gotta go."

Feeling relieved, I smoothed my dress back into place. "No

problem. I guess I should head home anyway, in case my dad comes home early. Sorry if I got you in trouble. Next time, I'll be sure to call."

"That would probably be best," he mumbled. And then he was gone, sauntering his sexy ass across the parking lot and back through the club's front door.

Evangeline held the door open for him, but didn't say anything as he passed. Instead, she watched me as I fumbled for the keys in my purse. I heard the door shut and felt a moment's relief until I looked up and saw that she was walking straight towards me.

Evangeline was beautiful. She seemed to be in her early thirties. She had silky brown hair, slate grey eyes, and a petite little frame reaching to only about 5'5". At one time I wondered if I should be jealous of her, but Christian had told me that she and Dax were involved and had been together forever. That had made me feel better. But right now, I was *not* feeling better...I was feeling nervous.

"Hi, Evangeline." I tried to sound light and upbeat. "Sorry for just showing up tonight. I truly thought the club was open or else I wouldn't have just walked on in."

Evangeline smiled. "Oh, that's okay. I'm sure Christian was happy to see you, and you're always welcome here Rose. We just aren't allowed to have any visitors before normal business hours. However, since we're going to be open in about thirty minutes, and even though you aren't twenty-one, I would be pleased to have you as my guest tonight if you'd like to join me."

I thought about her offer. It would be cool to finally enter the club and actually hang out, and to be the owner's guest would be great, but…"Thank you for the offer, but unfortunately I have to be getting back home." Yeah, I just wasn't feeling the love. Evangeline seemed nice and pretty sincere with her offer, but I could tell she didn't *really* want me there. And I truly did have to beat Dad home. This wasn't like one of his overnight trips; he was actually coming home tonight,

and I didn't even want to think about what would happen if I

wasn't there when he arrived.

* * * * *

CHAPTER FOUR

Christian

(Christian)

With the smell of blood in the air, and Rose's sexy body under my hands, I just couldn't help but nuzzle her neck a little more. She moaned a little as I started to lift her skirt, and that's when I heard, "Christian. I'm sorry to interrupt but we need to finish opening."

Really Evie…right now? Her voice carried the command that my brain needed to hear in order to stop where this was headed. I lifted my head and looked at Rose. She was flushed, and even though she tried to hide it, I caught the look of uncertainty that had flashed across her face. I'm sure she was questioning my darkening appearance, so I quickly tried to shake it off. I kissed her and headed for the club before she could notice too much…I hoped.

That was one of the things that sucked about being a vampire…no pun intended. When you started to "drift" from light to dark, your physical appearance actually showed traces of it. It's in our nature for us to drift from light to dark when we feed, when we're sexually aroused, or angry. Most of the time when the deeds are done and the emotions pass, we drift back to our natural state pretty quickly. These appearance traits made it easy to tell who was in control and who wasn't, but when they drifted in correspondence to our cravings, it could be a real pain in the ass.

As I rushed through the door, I almost ran straight into Terrance, who was being held in place by Dax and Bobby. He was on his knees, arms held out to his side, unable to move. I assumed Evie had commanded him to stay put before she made her way outside to get me.

"What the fuck did you think you were doing leaving this club to go feed in the woods?" I demanded. I had known exactly what he'd been doing the second I saw him. Terrance had come out of the woods with black hair and dark eyes. His usual coloring was a medium to dark brown. Because he was naturally darker we did tend to keep an eye on him, but apparently he had risen before the rest of us tonight so he could sneak out and have a bite. This is why Rose was able to get into the club. He could have grabbed Rose tonight instead of whomever it was he'd just left bleeding in the woods.

Now I was pissed. "Answer me, you asshole. You left this club wide open, and by doing so, you put us and our maker at risk. What if guests had shown up early tonight? They could have just waltzed right in and saw where all of us sleep."

"Like Rose did?" Evie asked as she came through the front door, her tone smooth as ice.

I had known I was going to have this conversation with her soon, but I had hoped it could wait until after we had dealt with Terrance.

"Rose didn't say anything about the stage." As a matter of fact, when we had first started dating, I bit one of her friends and used my sedative to convince him to describe it to her as a dance floor that moved on hydraulics, nothing more. "Evie, don't worry, she doesn't know a thing. She's innocent and if she *had* questioned it, she would have asked me and she didn't."

"I believe you Christian. I had a little talk with Rose this evening and I did a quick scan of her and you're right, she doesn't suspect a thing. But that doesn't change the fact that we could have had a serious problem if anyone *other* than Rose had showed up early tonight." Evie's gaze narrowed on Terrance.

Terrance tensed as he sensed the change in her voice. She was preparing to issue a command that he knew none of us would be able to resist.

"Dax, Bobby…escort Terrance back into the rising pit and chain him up in the cell. I will decide what to do with him after closing tonight. Oh, and Dax…make him sing."

Terrance visibly slumped when he heard her command. "Make him sing" were not words you ever wanted to hear her say.

Evangeline is our clan's Sire; Dax is her consort. They are the only two vampires in our clan that possess the ability to "scan" or invade someone's mind. They could choose to gently read your mind, barely probing your current thoughts, like she had done with Rose. Or, they could "make you sing." When they forcibly pulled thoughts from your head, it was not only excruciating, but you were forced to "sing" every detail of whatever it was that you were thinking without a choice. There was no way to hide your intentions or lie about what you had done. Terrance was screwed.

Dax and Bobby escorted Terrance back down to our actual

"rising" pit. This was the area where we all slept during the day. It was located far underground, beneath the club, and only had two entrances. One was under the circular dance floor, and the other was hidden behind a bookcase in Evangeline's office. I started to follow Dax and Bobby towards the pit, but just then Evangeline nodded her head in my direction. I guess we weren't done talking about Rose's appearance tonight after all. I followed her into her office and shut the door behind us.

"I like Rose very much," Evie started, "but I'm concerned that she is witnessing too much for her own good."

"You just said that you scanned her. If she had any questions or suspicions about me or The Rising Pit, you would have heard them then."

I wasn't about to let Evie ruin the best thing that had ever happened to me. Rose was the sweetest, most caring, and sexiest person I had ever met. The first night that I saw her leaning out of that limo and smelled her scent drifting on the breeze, I thought I'd died again. I recall writing her some cheesy poem in hopes of capturing her attention, but what I truly remember about that night was her scent. She smelled of innocence and sweetness: like fresh cotton and sweet tarts, and sunshine and rain, all mixed together. I was immediately in love with her.

"While doing my quick scan, I could sense something just below the surface: a wariness or apprehension of some kind. I'm just concerned that we may be the source of that," Evangeline stated.

"Or maybe it's because her mother was killed six months ago. And it probably didn't help that she was worried she'd gotten me in trouble, and then here comes the owner of the club making a trip across the parking lot to talk to her about it. Honestly, with everything she has gone through, I'd be surprised if she doesn't spend the rest of her life wary and apprehensive." I was feeling a little pissed and crossed my arms in defiance.

Evie cocked her head and took in my frustrated tone and

stance. A smile slowly spread across her face. "You're in love with her."

"Damn straight." I was not embarrassed to express my feelings for Rose in front of Evie. She and Dax had a wonderful relationship that made the rest of us long to have someone in our lives that we too could share eternity with. With Rose, eternity wasn't going to happen, but I didn't care. A lifetime with her was something that would sustain me until my true death. Yeah…I loved her that much.

"I haven't received any signs of the new Sire emerging, but when they do, you could always petition them to change Rose for you," Evie said.

I had never thought about Rose actually becoming a vampire. Mainly because *I* couldn't change her, and at this point neither could Evie.

When the Sire of a clan reached a certain age, their ability to share the life blood required for *the change* disappeared. A new

Sire within the line was eventually triggered to take their place, but sometimes that could take hundreds of years to happen. It had been eighty-five years since Evie last created a new vampire, and we hadn't had any signs of who the new Sire could be. Honestly, I thought we all had forgotten about it as our little family was pretty content.

"I hadn't even thought about it, but I guess when the time does come, I *could* petition the new Sire to change Rose." Hope was blooming in my chest.

Evie smiled, "Well it's certainly something to think about. I, for one, would welcome Rose with open arms. I've never seen anyone make you so happy and she does seem to be as sweet as you say. I think she would make a wonderful light vampire, and it would please me for you to be able to spend eternity with the person you love, just like me and Dax. "

"That would be amazing." I dreamily started to fantasize about an eternity with Rose.

Evie snapped my attention back to the present. "Now what should we do about Terrance?"

The air left my lungs. "Honestly, I don't know. He has always been a little darker than the rest of us, and even though we've monitored him successfully in the past, I really don't see him changing back this time. When he stepped out of the woods, his hair was black and his eyes were almost as dark, and I could smell and hear the woman he had left behind in the woods. She was bleeding, frightened, and whimpering. I could tell that Terrance had not made their interaction a pleasant one."

"Is that why you were *drifting*, because of the effect the woman in the woods was having on you?"

"Yes. With the scent of blood in the air, and Rose in my arms, I started to drift. Thank you for stopping me when you did."

I hadn't drifted in front of Rose before, mainly because I had always made sure to feed before she arrived. Plus, even if I did get really worked up, she usually had her eyes closed because she was just as into it as I was. But tonight she had shown up before I had fed and with the bleeding woman in the woods not far from us and her amazing body pressed next to mine, I hadn't been able to control myself. I just hope she hadn't noticed too much.

"I think I'll wait to hear what Dax gathers from Terrance and make my decision tonight after closing, as planned." Evangeline said, bring my attention back to the problem at hand.

As a rule, Evie didn't kill vampires just because they drifted from light to dark; it was in our nature and couldn't be helped. But she did have one strict rule: if any of us started to revel in hurting people and became permanently dark, we *would* face the true death. No exceptions.

It was very rare for a vampire to drift permanently dark, but it happened every now and then. When it *did* happen, it meant that they were giving into the darkness within them, which resulted in their emotions shutting down. That quickly led a vampire to start reveling in the kill and becoming truly evil. If it happened within a Sire's clan, it was their responsibility to deliver the true death. It looked like Terrance was out of time.

* * * * *

CHAPTER FIVE

Daddy's Little Girl

(Rose)

As I drove home, I couldn't stop thinking about Christian
and how great it felt to finally have him let loose a little. His
kisses were more intense and the way his hands moved over my
body was pure heaven. But there were other things that had
happened tonight that were occupying my thoughts as well. Like
my lying and scheming, my seeing Christian and his co-workers
coming out from under the stage, Terrance's sudden appearance
from the woods, and especially Christian's dark appearance and
odd mood swing. It's not that these things had exactly stressed
me out, but tonight had been so different from any of my other

visits with Christian; it all just felt a little odd.

But, odd or not, I really didn't have time to process it right now because I had bigger problems.

I was already running short on time, and had obviously gotten lost in my thoughts, because when I looked up, I realized that I had driven straight to my house in Jill's car. *Oh shit! What was I going to do now?*

I was supposed to have gotten a ride home from Ms. Culver after school, so how was I going to explain to my dad about Jill's car? I raced around the block, pulled the car up to the curb, eased it into park, then frantically dialed Jillian's number.

"Hey, where are you?" The tension was thick in her voice. Jill was waiting at her house, ready to jump in and drive me the rest of the way home.

"I screwed up!" I replied, sounding panicked, "I accidentally drove straight home instead of coming to get you. Is there any way you can come get your car? I'll leave it around the block to the east of my house with the keys under the floor mat. Is that okay?"

As the silence stretched, I really started to freak out. Maybe I had pushed my best friend too far this time. She was always looking out for me, especially since the nightmare with my mom, but this may have been asking a little too much.

"Okay, I think there is still one more bus that runs in that direction tonight. But Rose...you owe me big!"

After thanking Jillian profusely, I snapped my phone closed, turn off the car and put the key under the mat. I wasn't worried if it would be safe here or not, as we lived in a pretty nice neighborhood. As a matter of fact, my mother's death had been the only bad thing to ever happen here.

As I rounded the corner, I noticed that Dad's car wasn't in the driveway. *Thank God!* I just couldn't imagine how my dad would react if he came home to an empty house. Actually, I could imagine, and it scared the hell out of me. I pictured him being so scared that he called the police in a panic, or worse yet, having a heart attack and collapsing on the floor. I refused to put him through that, even if it did cut into my social life.

I went around the back of the house, let myself in, and headed straight for the kitchen. How was I going to explain the lack of food, when I was supposed to have had the driver stop for takeout? As I rummaged through the refrigerator, I heard Dad's keys unlocking the front door. *Shit, shit, shit.* I quickly shut the fridge, turned on the faucet, and began washing my hands just as Dad came around the corner and stopped in the doorway.

"Hi honey, how was your day?"

I wondered if the driver had given him the heads up regarding the change of plans after school. I was pretty sure that he had, so I decided to stick with that for the basis of my story.

"Not great. I wasn't feeling well today, and because of it I ended up having to stay after school. But Ms. Culver was nice enough to give me a ride home."

As he looked at me with a tilt of his head, I started to panic. "Yeah, that's what Dennis told me. So what's with the get up?"

Oh good, he was just questioning my sundress, darker make-up and wavy hair. "Oh, nothing. Just being a girl. After I got home and ate something, I was feeling better, so I decided to clean out my closet. I've been trying on clothes and messing with my hair. I thought maybe I'd wear this the next time I go over to Jillian's. The whole family always goes out to dinner whenever I stay over," I said as my stomach growled.

"I think it looks great," he said, "and actually, I think you will be headed over to Jill's next week. I just have to confirm some arrangements for my business meeting in Masen, and then I'll let you know for sure."

"Okay, sounds good. Well, I'm gonna turn in. I want to make sure I get up early enough to have a decent breakfast. I think that's why I didn't feel good today. I just hadn't eaten enough."

God, I really couldn't stand myself.

"Okay, honey. Get some rest; I'll see you in the morning, and how about I cook this time? Give daddy's little girl a break."

And now I was feeling sick for real.

* * * * *

CHAPTER SIX

Second Chances

(Christian)

After the club closed, Dax came out of the rising pit and headed straight for Evangeline's office. They were in there for about fifteen minutes while the rest of us cleaned up the evidence of tonight's good time. As they came out, the puzzled look on Evie's face had me feeling cautious as she waved us over to join her.

"After receiving Dax's report, I've decided that I need to keep Terrance around for further questioning." Evie's voice was sharp and to the point.

This was a first. Evie usually didn't give second chances,

and as far as I was concerned, I thought Terrance had already been pushing it for a while.

"What did Terrance say?" Curiosity was getting the better of me.

"His revelations about tonight were exactly what we thought they would be. He woke and snuck out early, then made his way out to the interstate and sliced the poor girl's tire. When she glided her car to a stop along the woods, he grabbed her. He was not gentle and he planned to leave her for dead all along." At that last statement, the anger lacing her tone was so thick it almost left a bitter taste in my mouth.

"Then why are you letting him live?" I demanded. "His actions tonight not only put us in danger, but it's obvious that he is starting to revel in the kill."

Closing her eyes briefly, she composed herself. "Christian, please know that I have yours, and everyone else's best interests at heart when I make my decisions. There is something within

Terrance's mind that I have to explore before I can dispose of him," she replied calmly. "But once I get my answers, he *will* meet the true death."

I noticed Dax had been quieter than usual during our little meeting, and now his head hung even lower with Evie's last words. Dax had petitioned Evie to change Terrance when he found him back in the old world working as a blacksmith. There had been an accident that had left Terrance's hands terribly burned. With his livelihood ripped away, he had no way to support his family. But if he were to die, his wife could remarry and gain the stability she and their children needed. Dax had explained this Evie, and so the two of them with their caring hearts, decided to add Terrance to our clan, freeing both him and his family from a terrible fate.

"Terrance will remain chained in the pit until further notice. No one is to talk to him unless I or Dax say so." She didn't have to raise her voice or repeat herself, for the command in her voice was enough to paralyze us all into doing exactly what she

wanted. Another benefit to being the Sire. When the Sire gave a

command, the rest of us had to obey. It was a skill she didn't use

very often.

Evie headed towards the front of the club, taking Bobby

and Dominique with her. I assumed they were headed out to

gather the girl's body that was still in the woods and dispose of

her car. I walked over to Dax and placed my hand on his

shoulder. We'd been together for so long that I didn't have to

say a word in order to express my sympathy, but I thought I'd

better apologize for sounding so "pro-death" when it came to

Terrance. "I'm sorry. I really wish he would drift back to himself

so we could stop this."

He looked at me with sadness in his eyes. "He's not going

to. Since about six months ago, Terrance has had trouble drifting

back after he feeds. Evie and I noticed it and were keeping an

even closer eye on him than usual, but then this happened," he said, gesturing to the front door. "Not only is he terrorizing and killing his prey, but he has now lost all regard for the rest of the clan's safety. No...he's not drifting back."

"What happened that would cause him to change so much?"

"Not sure. But that's what Evie's gonna find out." With sadness in his eyes, Dax clapped me on the shoulder then walked away.

As I headed out to help Evie and the others, I thought I heard Dax say something else, but I couldn't quite make it out. I thought he'd whispered, "Man I wish I knew how he was keeping those thoughts from me."

Now I understood. Dax hadn't been able to pull *specific* thoughts from Terrance. That was highly unusual and now I could see why Evie wanted to question him further. And I couldn't wait to find out what she discovered.

* * * * *

CHAPTER SEVEN

Business Unusual

(Rose)

The following week went by fast enough. I didn't get into anymore trouble at school, and now every morning Dad made sure I had a good breakfast so I wouldn't get sick again. *Yes, I know...I made that bed, and now I was lying in it.* I talked to Jill and made sure she had retrieved her car with no problems, which she had, and I was scheduled to stay with her again this Friday night.

That was the topic of our recent conversation. She made sure to tell me that this Friday night was when she would be collecting on the favor I owed her. *Great! This didn't sound good.*

Friday night arrived, and as I waved goodbye to my dad as

he pulled out of Jill's driveway, her hushed voice drifted to my ear. "If I'm going to help you sneak out to see Christian again, you are going to take me with you!"

That wasn't what I had been expecting, but as I couldn't see any harm in it, I happily agreed. "Okay, sure. I think that could be fun. And, since you are twenty-one, you can actually go inside while I'm, *ahem*, occupied with Christian."

After explaining to her parents that we wanted to skip dinner so that we could take in a double feature at the movie theatre, we began to get dressed and I realized that this was going to be the most time that I've been able to spend with Christian in months. Usually, I had to wait for Jill's parents to fall asleep, and then with her help, sneak out without waking them, setting off the dog, or tripping the flood lights. Once all this was accomplished, I would only have a couple hours to get there, see Christian, and get back. But tonight, we had checked the movie times, and after taking our drive time into account, we had gotten the okay to be gone for about four hours.

Honestly, I really didn't know what Christian and I were going to do to fill the time. I mean, don't get me wrong, I had plenty of yummy ideas of what I could do with Christian if we were alone for that long, but it wasn't like he could take a four hour break. With me still being twenty and not able to legally enter the club yet, I was thinking tonight would be the perfect time to take Evangeline up on her previous offer. I just hoped she was still in a generous mood or else I would be stuck outside in the car for about three hours, while Jill and Christian were both inside without me. *Yeah, that would suck.*

Jillian's question shook me out of my thoughts. "Does this look okay?"

Jill was on the volleyball team at school and had a great, athletic body: lean and muscular, with minimal curves and a small chest. So when I turned around, I was shocked. First off, I noticed that Jill had darkened her makeup quite a bit from the last time we were in front of the mirror, and her dark brown hair was now hanging loose instead of pulled up at the sides like before. Secondly, I didn't even know she owned clothes like this. It was like I was looking at a stranger. She wore a red leather miniskirt and a silver sequin halter, with a long, black, scarf-like duster over it, and knee-high black boots. "Um, yeah! You look really hot actually." I tried not to sound as stunned as I felt.

"Cool. The last time I was in that club was to go pee after that concert, and I tell you what...the people in there just oozed sex. I just want to make sure I fit in."

Huh, I guess I had better rethink my outfit. I had never really thought about the patrons of The Rising Pit, as I was always in my own little world with Christian in the backseat of his car. But I had to admit, her comment sparked a bit of insecurity in me. Maybe I should be more worried about the people who surrounded Christian night after night. What if I wasn't the only girl he made out with in the back of his car? Now I felt nauseous. "I'm going to go change."

After trading my plain jeans and tank top in for a black, sleek fitting dress and heels, Jill and I made our way out of the house without being spotted by her parents. We voiced our goodbyes and headed out the front door.

We were ten minutes away from the club when Jill, with a hint of teasing in her voice asked, "So, have you and Christian done the deed yet?"

"No, unfortunately," I huffed. This was something that I hoped we would remedy soon, but again, the idea of finally being that intimate with my boyfriend in the backseat of his car wasn't exactly at the top of my "most romantic moments" list. But at this point, I was getting desperate, so it might just have to do.

"Well, maybe if Evangeline lets you in tonight, you and Christian can sneak in one of those private booths they have upstairs and finally seal the deal," Jill laughed.

"How do you know there are private booths upstairs?" I was curious because I had never been inside long enough to really take everything in, and I didn't think she had either.

"When I was in there to use the bathroom, someone was talking about the private booths upstairs, saying that she wished she could get an invitation or something. I just thought that since Christian has access, it would be the perfect place for you guys to score some alone time tonight!"

Suddenly I felt a rush of sexual energy pulse through my veins. "Well, *if* Evangeline lets me in tonight, I think you're right; a private tour sounds like the perfect plan."

After we parked and Jill went inside to let Christian know we were here, I kept thinking about what she had said about those private booths. I mean, I know that the club had a reputation for being a very sultry place, but honestly, I had never really spent much time thinking about what went on in there. As I looked up from my ponderings, I saw Christian walking towards me. *Damn, he's sexy.* Suddenly, I hoped that what I had in mind was *exactly* what went on inside.

"Hi gorgeous!" he said.

Christian's kiss effectively weakened my knees, so I had a hard time concentrating on what he said next.

"I've got a surprise for you. Evie said that from now on you're welcome in the club whenever you want, as long as you wear this bracelet. She had it made for you after checking with the liquor board."

He had a big smile plastered on his face as he continued, "They said as long as she made sure that you had something to clearly designate that you're underage, you'd be able to join us."

I looked down at the black rubber bracelet; it had the club's logo on it, and the words UNDER 21 in white print repeated around the band. This I could live with.

"This is great, but how did Evangeline know that I wanted to come inside the club tonight?" I asked.

"I think she decided to have it made after the last time you were here. Actually, she had a bunch of them made. I think she's planning to bring in some extra revenue by opening the club to 18+ kids a couple of nights a week." Then with a fake pout he said, "I'm just not sure I'm ready to share you with everyone else though."

He pulled me close, placed his hands on my hips and looked straight into my eyes. "I like having you all to myself."

Suddenly I was feeling flush. I couldn't tell if it was from his sexy tone, or if it was just because I was so damn horny, but it didn't matter. Because just then, Jill stuck her head out of the front door and yelled, "Hey you two, get in here!" Christian smiled and took my hand, and as we made our way to the club's front door, I took a deep breath and thought...*I don't like sharing you with anyone else either!*

The club was dark and sexy. A thin layer of smoke drifted in the air as different colored lights pulsed from all different directions. The music was sensual and had a very bump-and-grind beat to it. The guests were just as Jillian had described them...oozing sex. There were amazingly beautiful women and men dancing and making out everywhere I looked. Suddenly, I didn't like the idea of Christian working here anymore.

"Come on, Evie wants to talk to you!" he yelled into my ear.

As we made our way toward Evie's office at the back of the club, I kept getting a weird feeling that everyone was watching me. I was used to people staring since I was pretty tall and had a very curvaceous figure and my blonde hair always seemed to attract attention. But this was different. It was like they were waiting to see what I was going to do...or what Evie was going to do to me.

As we entered Evie's office she gracefully rose from her chair. "Hello, Rose. I'm so glad that we could accommodate you tonight. I'm sure Christian already told you, but I want to extend my invitation personally. You are welcome at The Rising Pit whenever you want as long as you wear your bracelet."

"Thank you so much Evangeline." I had never felt comfortable calling her by the nickname Christian and everyone else used for her. "I really appreciate you thinking of me. I'll be turning twenty-one in just a few months, and until I move out of my dad's place I won't be down that often, but this is such a generous thing for you to do in the meantime."

"You're moving out? When?" Christian suddenly sounded serious, and not very happy.

"Well, yeah. As soon as I graduate college, which will be at the end of May, remember? I told you–I'm graduating early because of all the AP classes I took in high school. I only agreed to live with Dad as long as I was in college, and since that time is almost up, I'm ready to start looking for a place of my own." I felt slightly annoyed and more than a little confused by the change of subject.

Christian seemed upset at my news and I couldn't

understand why. I thought he would be happy that I would be out on my own and able to see him whenever I wanted.

Frowning, he continued, "I don't like the idea of you living alone. Not after what happened to your mom."

And now my evening was ruined. "Oh, Jesus Christ. Really? You sound just like my dad. Do you think the guy who killed my mom has been keeping tabs on me this whole time? What, has he just been waiting for me to move out, biding his time until he could strike? Be realistic, Christian. Just because I've had to face tragedy in my life, doesn't mean I'm different from any other twenty-one year old living on her own. Besides, I'm tougher than you think," I spat as I headed towards the door. "Thanks again for the kind gesture Evangeline, though it looks like I won't be needing it tonight after all."

I spotted Jillian at the bar as I rushed out of Evangeline's office. I realized that she had just had a drink placed in front of her when I grabbed her arm. "Sorry, change of plans...let's go."

* * * * *

CHAPTER EIGHT

Ruined

(Rose)

Just as I reached the club's front door, Christian grabbed my arm. "What's wrong with you?" His face was lined with genuine concern. Christian and I had never fought before. This was his first taste of my temper, and right now it had just started to boil.

"What's wrong is that I'm sick of everyone treating me like a fucking kid," I screamed over the bass of the music. "You don't seem to think I'm a kid when your tongue is down my throat or your hand is up my shirt, now do you?"

Taken aback, he gasped and dropped my arm. After a moment, he cocked his head towards the door. "Let's go outside." He walked out, leaving me standing there wondering if we'd survive our first fight.

I glanced at Jillian who was standing there watching me with a concerned look on her face. I leaned in and raised my voice enough for her to hear, "I'll be right back." She nodded and headed back to the bar to reclaim her seat and drink.

After I passed through the door and popped my ears, adjusting for the void of the loud music, I spotted Christian leaning against his car. His eyes were locked on mine as he tracked me from across the parking lot.

"I don't understand why you're so mad." Thick emotion laced his tone. "I love you, and it's only natural that I would be concerned and worried about you."

Listening to him express his feelings so openly made me realize that I had just ruined our entire night. Feeling ashamed I whispered, "I'm sorry. After all these months of my dad babying me, I guess I'm just overly sensitive to anyone who tries to coddle me."

He took my face in his hands. "Rose, I'm not trying to coddle you. I'm just worried about you living on your own. I'm your boyfriend, I love you, and that gives me the right to be concerned."

He loves me. As the fact settled deep in my bones, a warm feeling started to spread in all the right places. I pulled his hands away from my face and stepped closer. "Can we talk about my moving out later?" I reached up and laced my fingers through his hair. "I just really need to be close to you right now."

I didn't wait for his response. I leaned in and brushed my lips across his. When I pulled back to gauge his reaction, his eyes were closed and his breath was shallow. He licked his lips and then that sexy smile of his started to crook the corners of his mouth.

He opened his eyes, pulled me into his arms, and hugged me tightly. "All I ever want is to be close to you," he whispered in my ear.

I wrapped my arms around his broad shoulders and started to kiss his neck. He reacted by running his fingers through my hair and tilting my head so he could do the same. Feeling his lips and tongue slide along my skin made me break out in goose bumps. He leaned away, looking concerned. "Are you cold? Do you want to go back inside?"

I didn't...not really. I just wanted to stay out here in the dark, where Christian and I were the most comfortable. But I knew I needed to get back to Jillian, and Christian needed to get back to work. After kissing him once more I said, "Yes, let's go." I'm sure I sounded disappointed.

After Christian double and triple checked that I was okay, I convinced him to get back to work while I found Jillian. She hadn't been in her seat when we returned and her drink had already been cleared from the bar. After waiting my turn, I flagged down Dominique, the older of the two sister bartenders.

"Did you happen to see where my friend went?" I had to yell to make sure she could hear me over the loud music.

She nodded her head "yes" and then gestured towards the bathroom.

"Thanks," I yelled back in appreciation. I didn't know Dominique very well, but during the few run-ins we'd had, she'd always been really nice.

I headed towards the bathroom to make sure Jillian was okay. Once inside, I called her name, but there was no response. After checking under the stalls and verifying that they were all empty, I headed back out to the dance floor.

Looking around, all I saw were the patrons of the club, lost to either the beat of the music or the throes of passion. Finally, I glimpsed a speck of red out of the corner of my eye. Jillian, in her red leather miniskirt, was currently making her way up the curved staircase that lead to the club's second floor. And she wasn't alone.

Pushing through the crowd, I struggled to keep my eyes on her and her mystery companion, but kept losing them as I elbowed my way to the base of the staircase. When I finally broke through the crowd, I glanced up just in time to see them dip behind a curtained entrance. Just as I started up the stairs, Evangeline appeared, placed a hand on my arm, and motioned for me to follow her.

I really wanted to head up those stairs to make sure Jill was okay, but I didn't think it would be a good idea to refuse Christian's boss. Feeling frustrated, I followed as she led me to her office, held the door open, and motioned me inside.

"Are you okay, Rose?"

"Yes, I'm fine." I tried to sound as convincing as possible.

"I'm sorry that Christian's concern was upsetting to you. He tends to wear his heart on his sleeve, and as with most men, that can often translate into a fierce protectiveness. It's obvious that he's very much in love with you." She sounded more like his mother instead of his boss.

"I love him, too." I replied softly. This wasn't exactly a discussion I thought I would ever be having with Evangeline, but suddenly it felt good to have someone to talk to about this. "I'd do anything for him. That's why I thought he'd be happy I was moving out. We'll be able to spend so much more time together."

"I'm sure that he'll come around. As a woman who's lived alone for years, *I* know you'll be fine, but it's always hard to convince the men who love us that we don't need them 24/7," she joked. "Why don't you go wait for him at the bar? I'll go let him know that he can take his first break."

As we left Evie's office and headed towards the bar, it took me a moment to muster up my courage. "Would it be alright if Christian gave me a tour of the club? Since it's officially my first time inside, I'd really love to see more of the place."

After hesitating briefly Evangline said, "Yes. I think that'd be fine. I'll send him right over to you."

Just as I sat down, Tori placed a drink in front of me. I waved my bracelet at her. "Thanks, but I'm not allowed."

"It's just soda!" Smiling she headed back towards the man who was struggling to get her attention. Right then, I made a conscious note to myself; once I moved out and could come here more often, I would definitely be getting to know her and Dominique better. They seemed like a couple of really cool chicks.

As I sat there waiting for Christian, I kept thinking about Jillian and what the hell she could be doing up there with a complete stranger. Not that I didn't have any ideas. She was older than me and more experienced, but she was my best friend and I had brought her here, so yeah...I was feeling a little overprotective I guess. How ironic.

"So I hear I'm to give you a tour." Christian's smooth voice floated to my ear.

"Yes, you are." I slid off my stool and into his arms. "Let's start upstairs." Yes, I wanted some alone time with him, but this was also where I had last seen Jill. Two birds with one stone and all.

As we rounded the top of the staircase, I heard noises that indicated that everyone in this vicinity was having a *really* good time. "What are all these curtained off areas?" I had a feeling I already knew the answer.

"These are our private rooms. VIP guests can invite patrons to join them up here for a more *intimate* party of sorts." He sounded a bit hesitant in his explanation. I think he was nervous about how I would react. He probably thought I was going to be mad, which I might have been if Jill hadn't planted her wicked idea in my head earlier tonight.

"Are any of them empty so we can have a more *intimate* party of our own?" Tilting my head, I batted my eyelashes and let a sexy grin slowly play across my mouth. Christian's chest expanded as he took a deep breath, a feral look settling on his

face. He took my hand and began leading me to a private room

all the way at the end of the hall. That's when I heard Jill scream.

CHAPTER NINE

Damaged

(Rose)

I spun around and ran towards the room that I had seen Jill

disappear into. Just as I was about to reach for the curtain,

Christian was in front of me, pushing me back. "Let me by!" I

screamed. "That was Jillian and she's in there with some strange

guy!"

"It's my job, Rose. Let me do it." He looked serious, and as

I started to protest, I saw Dax bound up the stairs and give

Christian a quick nod.

"Let's go," Dax said.

Christian placed me by the railing. "Stay here. I'll bring her right out to you."

I gripped the railing so hard that my knuckles turned white. *Damn it, I knew I should have followed her up here.* I heard some rustling and low voices, but no more screams. I guess that was a good sign. Suddenly, Jillian appeared from behind the curtain with a napkin pressed to her neck.

I rushed to hug her. "Are you okay?"

"Yes I'm fine. I broke a glass and a couple stray pieces flew into my neck." She pulled away the blood-soaked napkin revealing two small, bloody dots.

"Oh, thank God. I thought that strange guy was raping you or something."

She laughed. "He's not strange and he's no stranger. I've known Justin for a while."

I should have felt relieved, but instead a layer of annoyance settled over me. "How do you know him? I've never seen him before. Does he go to our school?"

Dabbing at her neck again she said, "No. He doesn't go to our school. I met him in the yoga class I take at night over at the gym."

"Yoga? Since when do you take yoga? And what would a guy like that be doing in a yoga class?" I could tell by the look on Jill's face that I had sounded sarcastic.

"Picking up pretty girls of course," a smart-assed voice replied. I looked up to see *Justin* as he made his way out of the private room with Christian and Dax following closely behind. He was definitely Jill's type: longer blonde hair, blue eyes, great body. *Wow. Yoga does a body good!*

"Hi, I'm Justin." He extended his hand, which I did not take.

I'm not sure why I felt so pissed towards this guy, but I did. "I'm Rose, Jillian's best friend. So exactly how long have you two known each other?"

"About four months." Jillian's tone was clipped. I could tell she thought I was being rude. *Too bad.*

"Huh. Four months and I've heard nothing about you." I turned to stomp towards the stairs.

"Hey, what's wrong with you?" Jill grabbed my arm. "When you were outside throwing your hissy fit, I ran into Justin. We danced and then he invited me up here. We were having a good time, then I broke a glass and screamed. Next thing I know Christian and this brute," she flicked a thumb towards Dax, "come busting in. And now here you are being all shitty. What's up?"

I didn't have an explanation for her. I should have been relieved that she was okay, but instead I felt angry and annoyed. Right as I started to let my temper loose for the second time tonight, Christian eased up beside me and placed a calming hand on my lower back. It was just what I needed.

I looked at Jill who had gravitated towards Justin. Once I took a moment to really process the scene, I could tell that he was worried about her. He was holding her hand in one of his, and with the other, reached up and slipped fingers under the curtain of her hair and started massaging tiny circles at the back of her neck.

I exhaled a breath to calm myself. "Look, I'm sorry. It's just when I saw you disappear with someone that I *thought* was a stranger, and then I heard you scream...it just really scared me." Feeling embarrassed, I tried to play it off. "I guess Dad's over protectiveness is starting to rub off on me a little." I couldn't tell her why I was really upset...I couldn't tell anyone.

"Why don't you and Justin join us so I can get to know him a little better?" After almost blowing it with Christian, and now with Jillian, I wasn't sure it was possible, but I really wanted to try to end tonight on a high note.

Just then, I caught Justin eyeing Christian who had just exchanged a brief look with Dax. "Thank you, but I should really be going." Justin kissed Jillian on the cheek and darted down the stairs. Now I really felt bad because I had just chased off my best friend's boy toy for the evening. Can you say cock-block?

Just as I started to ask Christian if we could head back downstairs, Dax nudged his shoulder. "Can I speak with you privately?"

"Sure," Christian replied. Kissing me once more, he left Jill and I standing alone at the top of the stairs. *Awesome.*

* * * * *

CHAPTER TEN

Visitors

(Christian)

After kissing Rose once more, Dax and I ducked back into Justin's private room. This was always the one he reserved for his visitors. Justin was a vampire from a clan that resided just east of Masen.

Evangeline had made it a point to let all the vampire clans in the area know that they were always welcome at The Rising Pit, as long as they followed her rules.

Rule 1: Don't feed in public.

Rule 2: Make each feeding pleasant for your guest.

Rule 3: Make sure your guest doesn't remember.

Rule 4: *Never* kill.

Simple enough. There had never been a problem with anyone following the rules. On average, there were only about six or seven vampires that visited per night, and since there were fifteen private rooms, that always meant there was a private place available for them to feed.

Making their visitor's experience pleasurable was just as easy as making them forget. Every vampire has a "sedative" that flows from their fangs; the instant that they pierced a vein, all they had to do was *program* their desires into that sedative. Tonight it was obvious that Justin's sedative had worked in order to make Jillian believe that she had been cut by stray shards from a broken glass.

"That was close," Dax bluntly stated.

"Yeah, I know. I would have never imagined that the one person Justin decided to feed on tonight would be Rose's best friend. What are the odds?"

"Well actually, the odds are pretty good." That sounded ominous. "I scanned Justin and the best friend. She was telling the truth. She and Justin do know each other; apparently he feeds from her all the time. Yoga is the cover story if you hadn't guessed."

Damn. How was I supposed to keep Rose from learning my secret if she was not only going to be moving out and coming here more often, but also had a best friend that was the chosen guest of one of our regular vamps. Man, this sucked.

"Justin really does like Jillian if that helps at all." Dax was trying to make me feel better. It wasn't working.

Just as we finished cleaning, the curtains parted and Evangeline walked in. "Did we have a problem? I saw Rose and her friend outside."

"No. No problem." Dax kissed her on the cheek. "We were just cleaning up Justin's mess. What I got from my scan was that when things had gotten a little hot and heavy between him and

Jillian, she screamed in delight. Then he heard Rose and Christian coming, and that's when he broke the glass to use as his cover."

"That was quick thinking on Justin's part." Frown lines appeared on Evie's forehead, evidence that she was concentrating on something else. Suddenly her eyes widened and her head snapped in my direction. "How does Rose know Terrance?"

"What?" I was shocked, then I realized that she was scanning the girls outside as we spoke.

"I'm scanning Jillian and her memory of the evening is just as you described. She knows Justin from 'yoga'. They were making out up here, and then she broke a glass, sending pieces flying into her neck. What I don't understand is why I just saw an image of Terrance float through Rose's mind." Evie stared at me.

"I have no idea." I was starting to feel panicked when I

suddenly remembered that she had been with me when Terrance broke out of the woods the other night. "She saw him coming out of the woods the other night, remember?"

Evie stood silently for a few more moments. "Right now, she's thinking of everyone she's met here: Dom, Tori, us, and though Terrance flashed through her mind just a moment ago, he's no longer present in her subconscious."

Relieved, I sat down on the couch. "I just wish that we would get a sign of the new Sire already. I'm so sick of keeping my life from her. I want to tell her the truth."

Evie made her way over to the couch and sat down beside me. "I know it's hard Christian, but until you have approval from the new Sire that the change will be made, you know you can't tell Rose about us."

I knew she was right, but I just couldn't help thinking how much easier it would be if Rose knew about us. I couldn't wait to start making plans with her, maybe even move in together. And the best part was, I'd finally be able to feed from her. But that just wasn't going to happen any time soon. "Are we done here? I need to get back to Rose."

"Yes, we're done." Evie looked sympathetic as she took Dax's hand and headed towards the curtained exit. "I feel so bad for him," I heard her whisper.

"Don't feel bad for me Evie. I know it will all work out soon."

Suddenly, she whipped around and launched herself directly at me, grabbing me by my shirt as she slammed me down onto the couch. "What the hell?" I yelled.

The curtains flew open, and I saw Rose and Jillian standing there, trying to take in the scene before them. I was lying on the couch as Evangeline hovered over me, both hands wadded in the front of my shirt.

"What the hell's going on here?" Rose demanded.

Evangeline stared deeply into my eyes before smoothing the

front of my shirt back in place, and then she plastered a smile on her face. "Christian just saved me," she said as she righted herself. "My heel snapped and thankfully he broke my fall."

I looked at Evie and got the distinct feeling that something major had just happened between us, but I truly had no idea what it was, and now was obviously not the time to find out. She bent down and removed her shoe, which did in fact have a broken heel. After apologies and polite goodnights, she and Dax left the room.

Rose turned back to me with a skeptical look on her face. I remembered that she had questioned Evie and my relationship when we'd first started dating. I had told her the truth then; that she was the only one for me and had nothing to worry about. And I was going to tell her the truth now; I was in love with her and only her. But right now, instead of telling her, I just really wanted to show her. "Jillian, could you excuse us for a few minutes?"

* * * * *

(Rose)

Jillian took Christian's hint and left us alone. "What really happened with Evangeline?" I asked. I didn't like that I was questioning Christian, but walking in here to find him sprawled underneath his gorgeous boss on the couch, had really set off the jealousy bugs in my brain.

"Rose, I promise nothing strange was going on. Dax and I were cleaning up the broken glass and she came in to check to make sure everything was okay. She tripped on something and then the next thing I knew...boom; we landed on the couch."

I guess I believed him; I mean Dax *had* been standing right there. "Alright. I believe you." I sat down on the couch and let him pull me close. *Finally, time alone.*

It felt so amazing to be wrapped in his arms. He maneuvered me so I was lying on top of him. "Have I told you how sexy you look tonight?" he asked.

"No you haven't."

"Then how about I show you instead?"

Christian's kiss was sweet at first, but with the way his hands rubbed up and down my sides as I laid on top of him, it didn't take long for our passion to heat up. "I want you so much."

Christian's breathing was heavy and small moans repeatedly escaped his lips. "I want you too, Rose. More than you can possibly know. But we can't. Not here."

I was so disappointed. I was writhing like a snake on top of him and didn't think it would take much more for him to raise my dress and let me turn our private party into something truly intimate.

"Rose, you have to stop. You're driving me crazy, and I have to get back to work." Christian's voice carried a hint of laughter and a dash of frustration. I was glad that I wasn't the only one who felt frustrated.

We proceeded to make out for another few minutes until Christian's self discipline had him heading back to work for real.

"I don't want to leave." I sounded like a pouty twelve year old.

"And I don't want you to leave." Christian kissed me long and slow. "But you have to. Plus, now that you have your bracelet, you can come in whenever you have the chance."

"You're right, but it will still be only once a month until I'm able to move out."

The look on his face reminded me that he wasn't thrilled with this idea, but right now was not the time to discuss it. Plus, soon enough, he would see things my way. Everyone would.

* * * * *

CHAPTER ELEVEN

Terrance

(Evie)

"Evie, what's wrong? You seem distracted," Dax asked.

"I'm going to talk to Terrance. I'm still feeling uneasy about seeing him in Rose's thoughts tonight. I of course remembered that she'd had seen him coming out of the woods recently, but I had a gut feeling that there was more to it than that. I didn't mention anything before, because I didn't want to alarm Christian."

"How on earth could Rose know Terrance?"

"I have no idea, but you can damn sure bet that I'm going to find out." I turned and stomped towards my office to make use of my private entrance into the rising pit, leaving Dax to deal with the club's closing.

There were a number of things about tonight that had me feeling on edge: the strange image of Terrance in Rose's mind, the fact Rose's best friend ended up being Justin's chosen visitor, and the most shocking?; Christian had commented on something that I had *thought*–not said. I was so shocked when it happened that without even thinking I launched myself at him. The poor kid had probably thought I was attacking him but I wasn't. It had been almost ninety years since I lost my Siring ability, and if Christian was starting to hear people's thoughts that meant that he was developing powers. That was first sign of a vampire being triggered to become a Sire. I realized that I had overacted, but the thought of Christian becoming a Sire had jolted me. I just wish that I would have had time to explain that I was ecstatic at the development–not angry.

Could it really be Christian who was in line to become Sire?

My god, how amazing would that be? But oh, how I would miss him when it was time for him to leave us.

All new Sires were expected to leave their current clan in order to start a clan of their own. I would retain my powers and control over my clan, but I would lose someone that I loved very much. I couldn't think about that right now.

As I made the trek into the pit, I kept going over what I had glimpsed in Rose's head. I'd seen images of Dominique and Tori helping her at the bar, of Dax and Christian entering the private room together, and of myself sitting in my office. But then I had seen the image of Terrance. It had been just a quick flash that gave me no way to pinpoint the specifics and that was what really bothered me.

As I rounded the corner, I heard Terrance rattling his chains. I shouldn't have been surprised that he didn't like the idea of being alone with me. I may not look imposing or frightening to the naked eye, but since I was the one who decided if they lived or died, my clan couldn't help but fear me.

Luckily I had never been forced to kill anyone in my clan...yet.

I approached the cell which had no door, but instead a large

square opening that lead into the room. The walls were

composed of gray cinderblocks and had several sets of chains

mounted to them as well as to the ceiling and the floor. I realized

that this was the first time I had ever had to use them. It made

me sad. "Terrance. How are we feeling tonight?" His eyes were

locked on mine, radiating hatred. This wasn't a look I saw very

often. After all, we were family, and there was very rarely a

reason for discord among us.

"What do you want Evie?" Terrance's tone was laced with

contempt, "You already had Dax scan me, remember?"

"Yes, I remember. And I know that you're hiding

something. But I'm not here to talk about the girl in the woods.

What I want to know about is Rose." I had hoped the

abruptness of my question would shock him into revealing

something right away, but no such luck. It wasn't like I was an expert interrogator. So instead of catching a glimpse of any new information, I only picked up on our current conversation that was running through his head.

"Rose, who?"

"Rose Reynolds, Christian's girlfriend."

"Oh. The curvy blonde he's been dying to take a bite out of for months?" His tone was harsh and sarcastic.

"Christian loves her. He knows he can't feed from the one he loves without giving himself and his secret away. Do you love anything anymore Terrance?" I asked.

"Look at me Evie. I think you know the answer to that question." He was referring to his now permanently darkened appearance. It was obvious that he no longer felt love for anything and wasn't going to drift back. He was forcing me to inflict the true death on him. It's almost like he was asking me for it.

"Are you ready? Or would you like to see Dax one last time?" I couldn't help the quiver in my voice. I knew I had no choice, but Terrance was like a son to Dax. Back when I had turned Terrance, Dax had made it a point to watch over his wife and children, ensuring they were safe and well taken care of before we moved on. That had sealed their friendship for centuries.

"No. What's the point? Just do it." Terrance went slack and lowered his head.

The true death wasn't as horrific as it had been portrayed on TV or in any of the books people had read. In reality, it was quite simple. All I had to do was sink my fangs into Terrance's neck and program my sedative to carry the poison of true death into his system. Another power that resided only with the Sire. The poison would then spread through his veins, effectively paralyzing him as it hardened his body, eventually reaching his heart.

While the heart of a vampire no longer "beat," it was still the main energy source for their afterlife. Once the poison reached the heart, it hardened and withered, and then they simply turned to dust. No mess, no fuss...just dust.

As I approached, I could feel the tension drain from his body. He knew that this was the end. I gently placed my hands on his shoulders and guided us both down onto our knees. I looked into his eyes and then kissed him once on the cheek.

As I extended my fangs and lowered my head to his neck, I couldn't stop the tear that ran down my cheek and landed on Terrance's shoulder. He tensed as the evidence of my emotions ran down his arm. I felt a slight shudder move through him. *Finally.* When faced with the end of his existence, he started to show some emotion...and that's when I struck.

* * * * *

CHAPTER TWELVE

Questions

(Rose)

After I dragged out my goodbye with Christian for as long
as possible, Jillian and I climbed into her car and headed for
home. "Did you end up having *any* fun tonight?" Jillian asked.

Not really. But I didn't want to tell her that; she'd think it was
all her fault. "Sure, it was fun being able to hangout inside for
once, and spending time with Christian is always great." I tried to
sound convincing. It didn't work.

"Then what were you guys fighting about earlier?" She
looked at me with that *don't bullshit me* look on her face, that only
a best friend could pull off.

"He wasn't thrilled when I announced that I'd be moving out soon." My voice had gone flat. I understood that he worried so much because he loved me, but it was imperative that I got out of Dad's house as soon as possible. With everything that had happened–I just couldn't handle being there anymore.

"You'd think he'd be psyched that you're getting your own place. I mean, it's total freedom and you guys would get to see each other all the time. What's his problem?" *See, this is why I loved my best friend. She got me.*

"That's exactly what I was thinking, but when I told him and Evangeline, he just freaked and said that he didn't like the idea of me being out on my own." It still chapped my ass when I thought of him treating me like a kid. "But I know that once I have my place, he'll chill out and realize just how brilliant it is. We'll be together all the time. Together forever."

Jillian remained quiet for the stretch of a few miles. "I was hoping that we would be able to get a place together, but it sounds like you're setting up house for just you and Christian." Her voice was quiet and rang with disappointment.

"Oh! Well, I guess I hadn't thought much about a roommate. And you don't graduate college for another year and a half." Jill hadn't taken the AP courses like I had, so even though she was older than me, she was only in the middle of her junior year. "Plus, I thought your plan was to keep mooching off your parents for as long as possible," I joked.

"My parents aren't as strict as your dad, and I'm already twenty-one. If I want to move out I'm sure they will keep paying for college and everything as longs as I keep my grades up." She was certainly defending her case well, but with what I had planned for my future...I really couldn't have a roommate.

"I don't know Jill. Won't it be weird to be there while Christian and I are *together*?" I usually didn't mind talking to her about this kind of stuff. I mean we talked about sex all the time, but when it came to this, I really just wish she'd drop it.

"Um, haven't you ever heard of setting rules and using code? A tie on the doorknob, switching off days of the week, a certain colored hall light? Or, we could always just look for a place that had a great layout where the bedrooms were far apart. I'll be having Justin over too ya know!" *Wow...she was really picturing this happening.*

Snagging the opportunity to change the subject I said, "Tell me more about Justin. I can't believe you guys met at a yoga class. That's just so...strange."

"Why is it strange? I found the class when I was walking home one night after a volleyball game with Penny. We thought it looked fun, so we stopped in to grab a brochure, and as we were coming back out we ran into Justin."

"So he doesn't actually take the class? He just lurks outside of it?" This just kept getting better and better.

"What is your problem with Justin? Is it because I didn't tell you that I'd met someone new?" She was getting defensive.

"Like I said, we met about four months ago, but we've only gone out a few times. I guess I just didn't want to say anything until I knew how I really felt about him. And, honestly, before tonight we hadn't even made out." Her cheeks were red and she was breathing in small, tight huffs.

"And so, after one makeout session, you're ready to invite him into your house and make it more official?"

"Yeah. Actually I am." The look she gave me dared me to say anything else.

We rode the rest of the way home in silence.

* * * * *

CHAPTER THIRTEEN

Surprise

(Christian)

After we had all fed and finished closing the club for the
night, we started to make our way down to the pit. Dax and I
told everyone what had happened with Justin and Jillian. Their
laughter and jokes weren't helping my mood.

All my vampire brothers and sisters thought it was hilarious
that after 602 years I went and fell in love with a human. So,
anything that made my situation with Rose more difficult was
like the punch line of a joke to them: totally hysterical.

They continued to tease me and laugh as we made our way
to the bottom of the stairs. The circular enclosure that acted as

the top of our pit and the dance floor to the club settled in place with its customary boom. And that's when we all heard Terrance scream.

Dax glanced in my direction with a panicked look on his face. He took off in the direction of the scream and we all rushed to follow.

With our preternatural vampire speed, we all filled the opening outside the cell within seconds. Once there, we shared a collective sigh.

Evie wasn't delivering the true death to Terrance, but was instead looming over him with both of her hands clasped on either side of his face. He screamed again, just as Evie whipped back her head of jet black hair.

I'd never seen anything like this. I had thought she was "making him sing," but he wasn't "singing." No words broke his lips. Only screams.

Right as I saw Dax move forward, preparing to enter the

cell, Evie let Terrance go. He hit the ground like a drunk who'd finally reached his limit. Dax caught Evie just as she started to do the same.

Her hair immediately drifted back to its medium brown. She held his eyes for a moment and whispered, "There's a woman." Then she collapsed in his arms.

Dominique was the first to move. She helped Dax gather Evie then followed him to their room. Bobby, Tori, and I slowly made our way forward and could do nothing more than stare at Terrance lying on the floor, still in chains.

"So—who the fuck is this woman?" Tori's question broke the silence. It was laced with a bit of venom, as she and Terrance had been known to mess around occasionally.

"I don't know," I said.

"Well, I guess we're gonna have to wait until tomorrow to find out. The sun's almost up and I'm barely going to make it to my room as it is." Bobby waved us off as he headed down the hall.

We were your typical vampires. When the sun rose, we'd fall. Literally.

Even though the sun didn't burn us, once it rose we were rendered comatose and wouldn't rise again until it set.

Imagine if we got caught in a park or were walking along a road when the sun started to rise...you'd find tons of *dead* people lying all over the place until they *magically* got up once the sun went down. How the fuck would someone explain that?

So, for the protection of our species, all clans had secured lairs like our pit. And, like good little boys and girls, we all made sure that we were tucked in our beds before the sun came up. No one liked waking up on a hard floor or in a ditch somewhere.

The moment I hit the bed, I shut my eyes and thought of Rose. This was my ritual every night. She was always the last thing I thought about.

We didn't dream in our comatose state, but whatever we

thought of last would also be what we thought of first. I loved

that. Waking up to an image of Rose was pure heaven. Especially

the image I thought of as I settled down into bed.

* * * * *

(Rose)

When I woke up and didn't see my twinkling stars, I

panicked for a second. I always did that when I stayed over at

Jill's. It took me a few moments to realize where I was.

After our awkward ride home last night where Jillian was

mad at me for questioning her choice of boyfriend material, we

had gotten over it as we shared our customary bowl of ice cream

before going to bed.

Today was Saturday, so we didn't have school and I didn't

think that my dad would be home before 4 p.m. So once I

prodded Jill awake, I asked her if she wanted to go look at apartments with me. This was me trying to say I was sorry.

I still had no intention of rooming with her, but I would drop that bomb later. Right now, I just really wanted her with me while I scoped out my prospects. I was a little nervous.

The first neighborhood we drove to was only about ten minutes away from my house, and honestly, I wasn't sure I wanted to be that close to home. But it was a nice complex and was within walking distance of some really great shops and restaurants. That added some bonus points to my checklist.

As we drove up, I couldn't help but giggle. The complex was named "Tranquil Acres." It sounded like a fucking retirement home.

This was supposed to be one of the nicer apartment complexes in the area, and the business district would be a relatively short commute from here. Even though I didn't need money, as my mom's settlement would sustain me for most of my life, I was still was planning on getting a job after college. So being close to where I planned to work just earned this place another bonus point.

As Jillian and I headed towards the main office, I noticed a swimming pool off to my left. It was oversized and had wonderful landscaping. I had to pause momentarily, because I was having a severe case of déjà vu.

Suddenly, I found myself on the ground and Jillian was hovering over me. My breath was coming in rapid succession, causing me to hyperventilate. I was seriously close to a full-blown panic attack.

"Rose, my God, what's wrong?"

The complex manager was headed towards us and I tried to calm myself, but I wasn't sure I could. This pool reminded me of the one that my mom used to give swimming lessons in.

I didn't know why this was happening to me. My mom had been a swim instructor, and it wasn't like I hadn't been around pools since her death, but for some reason seeing this pool had me reliving more than I wanted to face.

"I'm so sorry." I repeatedly apologized to the complex manager as I raced my way back to Jill's car. I hated that I had made such a scene, but I really needed to get the hell out of there.

"What was that about?" Jill asked.

"I'm sorry I freaked out. That pool must have reminded me of where my mom used to give swim lessons." My voice was watered down with tears.

Jill leaned over and gave me an awkward hug in the car, "Oh, Rose. I'm sorry. Why'd you even put this one on your list then? Maybe we should mark off any complexes that have pools."

My voice caught on a sob. "I didn't realize something that simple could get to me so badly. Let's just get out of here."

I looked back and watched the pool fade into the distance

as we drove off. I couldn't believe that I had just had a panic attack because of a fucking swimming pool. But with everything that I had experienced with Mom during her lessons, I guess it shouldn't have come as that big of a surprise. Finding Mom being fed on by a vampire after one of her lessons was how I had come to learn that vampires existed.

* * * * *

CHAPTER FOURTEEN

Dread

(Christian)

I woke up and thought of Rose, just as planned. The image in my head was enough to start anyone's night out with a smile. But as I got dressed, a sense of dread slowly settled in my chest. I listened but couldn't hear anything out of the ordinary.

Maybe I was one of the first to rise. I hoped so I couldn't wait to meet with Evie and see what all that craziness last night had been about. After showering and dressing for my night, I headed out to locate Evie and Dax to see what was on the agenda for the evening.

I rounded the corner at the end of the hall to find

Dominique and Tori standing outside Evie and Dax's room with concerned looks on their faces.

"What's wrong?" I asked.

"Evie hasn't woken up," Dom replied.

Dax was sitting on the side of the bed, but as he got up and walked towards me, Evie's prone form was revealed. It looked like she was still comatose. "Something's wrong," Dax stated. "She hasn't actually woken up, but I can hear her thinking in my head when I scan her. It's like she is aware, but she *can't* wake up. I keep getting glimpses of Terrance feeding from some woman in the dark, and for some reason, this *really* has Evie upset."

I wasn't sure why this would be so upsetting to Evie. Feeding in the dark wasn't exactly *unusual* behavior for any of us. None of us had ever killed anyone or been discovered, so the fact that this particular scene of Terrance feeding was so upsetting to her was definitely strange.

"Anyone have any ideas of who this woman could be?" Dax

asked. "Has Terrance mentioned that he's been seeing anyone new lately?"

We all supplied a round of "No's" as our individual answers. Just then Bobby joined us. "Why don't we just ask Terrance?" he suggested.

"I already have," Dax replied. "After I couldn't wake Evie, I went straight to his cell and questioned him about what happened last night. Needless to say, he wasn't very forthcoming. As I scanned him, all I got were images of Evie and him locked in the same embrace we all saw them in. It was like he was trying to only relive that moment. It just kept repeating in my head like a record."

Dominique shook her head, Tori started to bite her nails, and Bobby just swore "Well, shit."

I hated leaving things unsettled, but we had a club to open. "Well, this is going to have to wait until tomorrow. We all need to head out to feed and get back in time to open the club."

Dax looked at me with a worried look on his face. Who could blame him? "I'm not leaving Evie. Christian, you're in charge of the club tonight, but come get me if there are any problems."

With our marching orders, we all scattered in different directions. As I walked past Terrance's cell, I glanced inside to find him with his back to the opening. *Whatever.* It wasn't like I wanted to talk to him anyway.

"I know it was her. What the hell did she do to me?" I heard Terrance say. His voice was like a whisper on the wind.

"Who the fuck are you talking about?" I turned around to confront him.

As he slowly spun around, I registered the strange look on his face. He just stood there...staring at me.

I asked him again, "What the fuck are you talking about? And, who did what to you?"

This time, he rose to his feet and took a couple of steps in my direction. "Can you hear what I'm thinking Christian?"

Frustrated, as it was obvious that he was fucking with me, I tightened my fists, wanting nothing more than to enter his cell to beat his ass for some answers. But, since Evie had commanded us not to go near him, I literally couldn't touch him. So instead I flipped him off and continued towards the stairs. *What an asshole.* I'd never really liked Terrance. Especially with the crap he'd been pulling lately: killing that girl in the woods, plus it was looking more and more like he'd done something to Evie while their minds were connected. I was really over this guy.

* * * * *

(Evie)

Dammit, what the hell had Terrance done to me? I was laying here trapped like a prisoner inside my own body. The last thing I remembered was leaning in and, pretending that I was about to deliver the true death,

feeling his mental shields give way, and that's when I struck. I was trying to

make him "sing" about the root of what had caused him to drift

permanently dark, but the second I found the image, he clamped his shields

back in place, and damn that had hurt.

No one had ever been strong enough to do that to me before, but then

again, it's not like I had to scan my people very often anyway. Maybe my

gifts were starting to fade since it looked like Christian was close to becoming

the new Sire. Who the fuck knew...but I had to wake up soon so we could

figure out who that woman was, and why in the world Terrance was afraid

of her.

* * * * *

CHAPTER FIFTEEN

Hiding

(Rose)

After my melt down at the apartment complex, Jillian drove
me back to her house and I cancelled all my other appointments
for the day.

"Are you sure you're okay?"

"Yes. I'm fine."

And I was, it was just a little startling to realize how much I
had blocked out about Mom. Apparently I had gotten very good
at hiding things...even from myself.

Once we got back to Jill's, I realized that I needed to do
some serious thinking. "Do you mind if I take a bath? I just need

to be alone right now."

"Sure thing. Let me get you a towel." Jill headed towards the linen closet, glancing back repeatedly with a concerned look on her face. There was no way I would be able to explain to her why I was so freaked so she was just going to have to continue to think I was missing my mom. Which was true, but honestly what I really needed to contemplate was how the hell Jillian had gotten mixed up with a vampire, and if I could use him to complete my original plan.

* * * * *

(Christian)

The club ran smooth, even though we were all on edge. After closing, as we headed back to the pit, we heard Dax's raised voice. "Tell me what you did to her!"

That didn't sound good. I guess Evie hadn't woken up. We

all stopped and continued to listen from around the corner.

"I didn't *do* anything to her, I swear." Terrance's low voice sounded tired and oddly enough, sincere. "I honestly thought she was going to deliver the true death and instead she scanned me, trying to force me to "sing." It hurt and all I could do was scream. I wish she had just killed me instead." He sounded so sad.

"What happened to you Terrance?" Dax was practically pleading. "Why can't you just tell me? We've been best friends for centuries. I've always known your darker appearance stems from the pain and sorrow you carry with you due to the loss of your family, but you never killed anyone and you've always drifted back...what changed? And how the hell are you hiding it from us?"

"I'm not hiding anything. I don't know why you and Evie can't scan my thoughts. Honestly, I don't know what has happened to me."

What was weird about this was that I actually believed him. As silence spanned the next few seconds, I motioned to everyone and we moved around the corner.

"Everything okay?" Bobby asked.

"No. It's not okay. Evie is still comatose, but I can still scan her thoughts and keep getting the image of Terrance feeding off a woman. It should be no big deal, but it's really upsetting Evie. And Terrance won't tell me who the woman is or why Evie can't wake up." Dax sank to the floor with his back resting against the wall and placed his head in his hands.

I'd never seen him this distraught, but who could blame him? I knew he felt helpless—we all did.

"I told Dax I don't know why they can't scan my thoughts. I'm not purposely trying to hold anything back. I can remember a woman, but I don't know anything about her. Whenever I think of her, things just get fuzzy," Terrance said, sounding defeated.

I'd never heard of anything like this before and I wondered if Evie had. Unless you'd gone through the ritual of being triggered and becoming a new Sire, no one else really knew a lot about the process or what went along with it. I was starting to wonder if her scanning ability had been weakened by the fact that she could no longer inflict *the change*. If Evie didn't wake up soon, I'd have no idea what we were going to do next.

Dax didn't seem to have a clue as to what was happening either. And from the looks of it, he was getting pissed. Suddenly, he pushed himself up off the floor in a burst of speed and had Terrance by the throat a second later. "I may not have the poison of true death, but I can still make you suffer."

I grabbed Dax's arms and tried to ease his grip on Terrance. "Hey, hey, hey...I think we should all just clear our minds and calm down. *Wait...maybe that's it!*

"Dax, you said that you can scan Evie's thoughts and see what's she's thinking, right?"

"Yeah? So?"

"Well, what I'm thinking, is that we need to try to use your scanning abilities to communicate with Evie. Since you're her consort, the bond you two share should not only allow you to scan her thoughts, but it should also let her scan yours."

Dax looked at me for a moment and I couldn't tell if he thought I was crazy or if he could see the brilliance of my plan. "Okay, so you're saying I should just think about how I want her to clear her mind and that should work?"

"Yes. Terrance said that when he thinks of this *woman*, his thoughts get all fuzzy. What if that's what's happening to Evie? Because she's so focused on her, maybe that's why she can't wake up."

Everyone stared at me like I suddenly had three heads. I couldn't explain it, but I just knew that this was the right thing to do and there wasn't a moment to waste. "Come on. We at least have to try."

As everyone headed towards Evie and Dax's room, I heard Terrance whisper again, "What did she do to me?" It was becoming glaringly obvious that we needed to wake Evie up fast and find out who this mystery woman was.

* * * * *

CHAPTER SIXTEEN

Ancient History

(Christian)

Dax sat down on the bed next to Evie while we all gathered

around the door. He took her hand, closed his eyes, and lowered

his head. I had told him to focus on giving Evie a clear picture

of letting go of her thoughts and clearing the image of Terrance

and this woman out of her head.

After a few minutes, Dax opened his eyes. "I think it's

working. When I scan her now I can see that she is trying to

focus on calming her thoughts and blanking out her mind. I

think we should know any minute whether it's worked or not."

We all stood there holding our breath, anticipation so thick it coated the air. Nothing like this had ever happened to any of us before and honestly, I think we were all a little scared that Evie might never wake up. This situation was quickly becoming fucked, but right then Evie's eyelids fluttered. She was fighting to wake up. Thank God.

"Evie?" Dax pleaded. "Come on honey, I know you can do this. Come back to me. Come back to us all." Dax was a big guy. He was muscular, had a buzz cut, and was a usually intimidating, but right now he sounded like a little kid who had lost his puppy. In my eyes it didn't make him any less of a man; it actually filled me with respect for him and the love that he carried for Evie. I felt the same way about Rose, and I knew that if anything like this ever happened to her, I would be acting the same way or worse.

Evie finally opened her eyes and took in Dax's face. She reached up and stroked his cheek. "Thank you my love," she whispered. "How did you know that clearing my mind would work?"

"I didn't. It was Christian's idea." Dax scooped her up into his arms and started kissing the top of her head.

Evie stared at me with a look on her face that I couldn't quite describe. There was a hint of gratefulness, a hint of curiosity, and a hint of respect. I wanted to rush in and start asking questions, but just then Dominique spoke up. "Why don't we give these two some time alone? The sun is almost up and we'll all be out again soon, so let's just plan to meet back here first thing after rising. If that's okay with you, Evie?"

"Thank you Dom. That would be great. I'll see you all after rising...and Christian, thank you."

I nodded my head and headed out the door towards my room. I couldn't wait until I had some alone time with Evie, because for some reason I had a feeling that there was more going on than just what had happened between her and Terrance. As a matter of fact, I still hadn't had the opportunity to ask her why the hell she launched herself at me in the private room. Yeah, we definitely needed to talk.

After making my way back to my room, exhausted from the nights drama, I didn't even bother getting undressed. I just laid down on the bed and thought of Rose as the darkness claimed me.

* * * * *

(Evie)

I watched Christian walk out my door as I relaxed into Dax's embrace. I had to figure out what all this meant. I needed to not only get to the bottom of what was going on with Terrance, but to truly confirm if Christian was the one being triggered to become Sire. It certainly appeared to be the case. He was able to hear my thoughts, and somehow he mysteriously had known that clearing my mind would work. I was actually starting to wonder what other traits he would start displaying. I tried to remember back to when I was triggered to become Sire, and these traits were definitely not things that had happened to me. But then again, thinking back that far was like trying to access ancient history.

Dax broke my train of thought as he twisted me around in his lap. "Are you truly okay Evie? I was worried sick and so mad that I almost tore Terrance limb from limb."

"I'm fine. Now that I'm awake, when I think about what happened all I get is the image of Terrance and I locked in our embrace. For some reason I don't see the image of that woman. It's almost like it's now blocked from me."

"Terrance said that he isn't purposely hiding anything from us. That when he thinks back to the woman you mentioned things just become fuzzy."

"I don't know what's going on, but Dax, I'll admit I was

scared. But now I'm pissed. Nothing like that has ever happened to me before. Something strange is going on and we need to figure it out fast."

Dax hugged me tightly. "We'll figure it out Evie. I promise."

I didn't doubt him; I never did. Dax was the love of my life, and for a vampire, that's saying something. It had taken 327 years for me to find the perfect man to become my consort. It happened in 1162 A.D. when I was in Ireland. I had been on my way to find a boat to the Americas, and that's when I had first seen Dax.

He was working at the docks, and for the first time since becoming a vampire, I actually felt out of control. The pull that I felt towards him was like gravity. He was so beautiful: his sculpted body, his buzz cut brown hair, and those sparkling brown eyes had me postponing my trip just so I could stay and watch him.

I followed him for three days, but after several silent trips back and forth through the shadows, I knew this was the man I wanted to share eternity with. He was masculine, kind, and had a great sense of humor. But I didn't think I could bring myself to actually kill someone and force them into a life with me without them having any say. The next day this concern was eliminated for me.

There was an accident on the docks. One of the pulleys that held the ropes that were used to lift heavy containers onto the ship broke. I watched in horror as the large wooden crate headed straight for Dax. He didn't move fast enough and it landed on him, crushing his legs.

I didn't take time to think, but instead used my vampire speed and strength to toss the crate aside, scoop him up, and run until we were safe in the woods outside of town, all of which took about ten seconds.

Dax was of course in shock, but after explaining what I was and how by changing him I could save his legs, he agreed to become my vampire consort.

* * * * *

CHAPTER SEVENTEEN

Bad Ass

(Rose)

After bidding Jillian goodbye and thanking her parents for having me yet again, Dad and I headed home. We had stopped for takeout on the way, and were now sitting at home finishing out our Saturday evening by eating Chinese food and telling each other how our weekends had gone.

"Did you have fun with Jill this weekend?"

I wasn't sure if Jillian's parents told my dad that we had "gone to the movies" or not, but I didn't think so. He had always been pretty good about trusting them to watch out for me, so I decided not to share this little tidbit. "Yeah, it was okay, we really didn't do much Friday night, but today Jill and I went looking at

apartments."

I knew this wasn't a topic that he wanted to ever discuss,

but too bad. After Christian and my little argument over it, I was

still feeling a little jaded about the subject. It was time I stood up

for myself, even if that meant having an argument with my dad.

Dad took a deep breath. "I know that you turn twenty-one

in April and then graduate in May. And I know I said that you

could move out once you had graduated. But Rose, don't you

think it's still a little too soon after everything that's happened?"

"I don't think so, Dad. I'm a responsible girl, and I know

Mom would want us to move on with our lives and that is

exactly what I'm trying to do." I set my fork down, shifted in my

chair, and met Dad's gaze. "I could have easily given up on

everything when she died. And there were times when I thought

I wanted to, but I didn't. Instead, I kept getting out of bed every

morning, I kept going to school every day, and I kept getting good grades so I could get a good job after college even though I don't need to. I want to live my life Dad, and that involves me growing up and moving out."

The more I thought about Christian and my dad having a problem with this, the quicker my temper continued to rise. "And if I can be honest here, I'm feeling really stifled with how protective you've become. You just said it yourself; I'm going to be twenty-one soon, and I really don't feel like I should be forced to have a sleepover every time you head out of town." I shoved the chair back from the table and stood up, continuing my rant as I cleared the dishes away. "As a matter of fact, I want to buy a car. I'm sick of being driven around by your guard dog for hire, or having to bum a ride with Jillian." I was on a roll. I wasn't sure where this newfound strength was coming from, but I was happy to have found it. It felt good to get all this off my chest. Dad, on the other hand, was looking at me like I'd just lost my mind.

He sat there stunned for a few moments while I leaned back on the counter. I had almost sounded like a badass; now I was trying to look the part. It didn't work.

"You know that I've always been proud of how you pulled yourself together after what happened. And I'm even prouder that you want to get a job after you graduate instead of living off of your settlement money. But that doesn't mean I will ever stop being your father, and with that comes the right to not only protect you from others, but to protect you from yourself. I just don't think you're ready to be out on your own yet." He finished with a very stern voice, stood up and dropped his plate in the sink with a loud crash.

My dad wasn't someone who showed anger very often, but I could tell that my little speech had pissed him off. "I can't believe you are coming at me with this kind of attitude. We haven't even had a single conversation about me buying you a car, or you moving out, and the first time you want to talk about it, you act like this? Not the brightest move, Rose."

"It looks like we are having a conversation about it right now! And I'm sorry if I have an attitude. I'm just trying to talk to you about my future, but for some reason you refuse to acknowledge that I have one! Plus, I don't need you to buy me a car, I can buy it myself!" Now I was the one who was pissed. "I'm so sick of being the sweet little girl who does just what Daddy says."

Dad opened his mouth as if he was about to yell back at me, then shook his head, took a deep breath, and slowly walked in my direction. "Rose, I'm sorry," he started as he placed both hands on my shoulders, "I just don't think I'll ever get past seeing you as my little girl. And you're right; you've been dealing with the brunt of the fear that I've been fighting since your mother's death, and it's not fair to you. How about on Monday I pick you up from school and we go car shopping? Then we can talk about this apartment idea of yours."

Wow. That was quite a turnaround. Not that I wasn't

grateful for the change in his perspective, but I had a feeling

things weren't going to go as smoothly as he was making them

sound. "Okay. That sounds great actually." I tried to keep my

voice steady and strong, when really, I was so excited about the

idea of getting a new car that I wanted to squeak and squeal.

Dad hugged me and moved off to put away his left over

Chinese food. I started to do the same when I heard a knock at

the front door. Dad's head snapped up from the table. "Are you

expecting someone?"

"No, are you?"

"No, I'm not. Get upstairs right now and don't come out of

your room, no matter what you hear." Dad's voice was clipped,

serious, and panicked. So much for making progress on his over

protectiveness. For all we knew, it could just be a couple of

Jehovah's witnesses, but he was acting like Satan was knocking at

our front door.

CHAPTER EIGHTEEN

Complications

(Christian)

It seemed like everyone had risen at the same time today. We had all gotten up and moved through our usual routines fairly quickly and arrived outside Evie's door at practically the same time. I thought it was pretty obvious that we were all still concerned over what had happened and wanted to see if Evie had indeed risen tonight without any further complications.

As we greeted each other with head nods, or slight shoulder bumps, we heard Evie and Dax talking from within. Thank God she was awake.

"Hey! Quit messing around in there. You've got a crowd of

concerned people waiting out here." Tori announced.

"Okay. Give us just a minute and then we'll meet you guys upstairs," Evie called out.

Bobby wagged his eyebrows. "I bet it takes them more than a minute if you know what I mean."

Everyone started laughing as we headed down the hall. Finding Evie awake and okay had definitely lifted our spirits. As we filed past Terrance's cell, we found him sitting on the floor, back resting against the wall. He gave us all a weak smile, then said, "I take it Evie woke up?"

Everyone stopped and looked at me. I guess since I was the first vampire Evie had sired after Dax, it kind of put me "higher up" in our ranks, even though we didn't really have ranks.

I gestured for everyone to head on up while I took a moment to answer Terrance and maybe ask a few questions of my own. "Yes, she woke up. We're heading upstairs to have a meeting about what happened."

"Would it be too much to ask for you to let me know how the meeting goes?" Terrance sounded calm and collected. I supposed I would too if I was trying to get information out of someone.

"Yeah, I don't know about that. Plus, you know that's something only Evie can decide."

It only took him a second to launch himself at me, rattling the chains until they pulled tight. His eyes were glued to mine and he squinted slightly. I thought he was trying to attack me, so I landed a kick to his chest that sent him flying back into the cinderblock wall. "What the fuck do you think you're doing?" Every time I got near this guy he did something else to piss me off.

He took a moment to right himself and stood with his back against the wall. "Huh. I guess I was wrong."

I started to stomp into the cell. "What are you talking about? Wrong about what?" I was so over this asshole. All I wanted to do was land a few more punches before he answered, but his next statement stopped me in my tracks.

"Wrong about the fact that you're going to become our new Sire." The deadpan look on his face was the only indication that he was serious.

"You really are fucking crazy aren't you?" I turned to walk away when I heard him call out, "You've read my mind before Christian, and you were just able to go against Evie's command. What do you think that means?"

Holy shit! I had just entered his cell against Evie's command. But me? Sire? I didn't think so. I hadn't shown any signs of developing powers, and Evie certainly hadn't reported that she had sensed I was the one being triggered. As for being able to enter the cell, I wondered if Evie's powers truly were fading. I was sure that it had nothing to do with me, and this was just another classic case of Terrance being his asshole self.

As I reached the top of the stairs and emerged out from

under the stage, I saw everyone sitting at one of the tables talking casually. Obviously, they hadn't noticed that Dax and Evie were huddled just inside Evie's office.

The two must have used the passage that lead from the pit to her office to enter the club, and by the look of things they weren't quite ready to get this meeting started. Dax was frowning and Evie was shaking her head back and forth. I didn't think they were arguing, but it was pretty obvious that they didn't agree about something.

"What did Terrance want?" Tori asked, pulling my attention away from the office.

"Nothing really, he was just being an asshole. He asked if we could tell him what happens in this meeting." I wasn't going to tell them about Terrance's ludicrous comment about me becoming Sire...what was the point?

"Yeah, right. Like that's going to happen. No way will Evie keep him updated on what's going on. Especially when what happened to her was his fucking fault." It was clear that Bobby

was having a hard time controlling his anger; his hair kept

drifting from blonde to brown and back again.

"Yeah, that's pretty much what I told him," I said.

Evie and Dax must have approached the table while Bobby

was talking, because just then I heard Dax say, "I think we

should deal with one thing at a time is all. Let's get to the bottom

of what's happening with Terrance first, and then you can

question Christian."

I turned around to ask what they would need to question

me about, only to find that they were still inside Evie's office.

Evie looked up and met my eyes just as Dax started out the

door.

Something strange was definitely happening here. All

vampires had the ability to hone-in and hear things from a

distance, but you usually had to make a conscious effort to do

so. And right now...my hearing had just zoomed in on

something without my control. By the look on Evie's face, she knew what had just happened and she was concerned about it.

Dax and Evie made their way over to the table and all the chatter quieted down. "I'll start by saying that I probably don't have the answers that you want, but I'll tell you everything I can remember," Evie stated. "First of all, I want you all to know that when I went down to talk to Terrance, I had no intention of delivering the true death, but when it became clear that he wasn't going to willingly give me the answers I was looking for, I decided to let him think that his time was at an end. At the last moment, I felt his mental shields give way, and that's when I struck. I tried to make him sing, and as you are all aware, that didn't work out very good for either of us." Evie looked around, making eye contact with everyone. "I want you to know that I had no idea that it would be so painful for Terrance. The last time I had to "make someone sing," they were weakened mentally and physically afterwards, but there was no evidence of actual pain. With Terrance however, you could tell by his screams that this was not the case."

I could tell this was upsetting for her. She sounded guilty and almost apologetic, even though she had nothing to be sorry for. Terrance had brought this on himself as far as I was concerned.

"The moment I penetrated his mind, I caught the image of him feeding off a woman in the dark. She was tall, thin, and had long, blonde hair from what I could tell. The moment that I locked on and tried to expand the image, Terrance's shield snapped into place, causing me a lot of pain, and then our connection was severed."

We all sat there in silence, none of us really knowing what to say. I had never heard of anything like this and from the quiver in Evie's voice, neither had she.

Bobby broke the silence by asking, "Did you recognize the woman?"

"No. I didn't. I was hoping that I could have picked up on a name or something more specific, but as soon as the image started to sharpen, it was over and I was being knocked out."

"Terrance says that whenever he thinks of that woman his thoughts go all fuzzy. Do you think that's the reason you were unable to wake up? Because of whatever weird effect this woman has on Terrance?" I asked.

"I've been thinking a lot about that, and it definitely seems like the most logical answer. But I just can't figure out how the woman could be affecting Terrance or me." Evie looked up at Dax and smiled sweetly. "I thought that Terrance had started reveling in the kill and had figured out a way to hide things from us, but now I'm not so sure. I almost think that he may be just as much a victim in this situation as the girl in the woods. I hope everyone can understand that I feel we need to keep Terrance around until we can figure all of this out."

Whether I was as convinced of Terrance's innocence or not,

I knew it would make Dax feel better if Terrance ended up not being the bad guy we all thought he had become, and that made me happy. "Is there anyone that you can contact to see if something like this has ever happened before?" I asked.

"Dax and I have discussed it, and we've decided that I should contact my Sire to see if he has ever heard of anything like this before. If something like this has ever been recorded, then I'm sure Balam will have heard about it. Now, let's go feed and get this club open. I know that this situation has everyone on edge, but I'm fine now, so there's no need to worry."

I wasn't as convinced by Evie's pep talk as everyone else was, but that was because of what I had accidentally heard her and Dax discussing. I was going to approach her about it, but then she and Dax started heading towards her office. I could only assume she was going to make the call to her Sire now and I certainly didn't want to delay that. We needed to get some answers as soon as possible. So instead, I headed out to feed along with Bobby, Dom and Tori.

We usually were able to charm a few people in the park nearby, taking only our fill and then making them forget. No harm, no foul. I, for one, couldn't stand the idea of hurting anyone, and it wasn't my fault that I required blood to survive. So like most vampires, we fed only out of necessity and didn't hurt anyone in the process. We were almost complete opposites to the vampires of legend, but I wouldn't change a single thing. I was happy in this life, and I knew everyone else in our clan, Terrance notwithstanding, felt the same way.

If Rose was eventually changed, I would be the happiest vampire alive...what a contradiction.

* * * * *

(Evie)

"Dammit, Dax! I know Christian heard us talking from inside the office. I'm telling you, he is displaying signs that he's the one being triggered. I need to talk to him about it."

"Evie, please. Let's get to the bottom of this thing with Terrance first. I will be just as happy as you if it is Christian that's being triggered, but right now you have to understand that I am a nervous wreck because of what happened to you. You have no idea what it was like sitting there next to you and not having a clue how to help. I thought I'd lost you." Dax pulled me close and I could feel him trembling slightly.

Dax was right. The situation with Terrance needed to be our first priority, but for reasons I couldn't explain I felt a strong sense of urgency about Christian becoming our new Sire, and I couldn't deny that it had me on edge.

CHAPTER NINETEEN

Good News

(Rose)

As soon as Dad heard the knock at the door he fell straight into panic mode, and for some reason, so did I. I was now listening for any noise that could identify our unexpected caller from behind my cracked bedroom door. So far, all I heard were jumbled voices.

After deep breaths and a few thoughts to convince myself that I was a badass, I started down the stairs when I finally heard something...a female giggle. *What the fuck.*

As I rounded the corner, I got a good look at the intruder. It was a woman with long blonde hair in a pencil skirt and heels.

And she had her hand on my dad's arm.

"Rose! It's okay honey. Please come here. I'd like you to meet someone." Dad's voice had sort of a high-pitched, panicky sound to it.

As I walked towards them, my dad took a step back and the woman turned around to face me. She was really pretty and had a Barbie doll smile plastered on her face. "Hi, I'm Meredith." I shook her hand thinking, *and I should care why?*

"Honey, Meredith is one of my clients from Masen," Dad explained.

Why would one of my dad's clients be at our house on a Saturday night? I didn't think I liked where this was going. "Didn't you just finish your meeting in Masen last night, Dad?" I asked, all the while keeping my eyes plastered on Meredith's.

"Yes, actually I did, so this is quite a surprise." He looked at Meredith and then gestured towards the living room with his arm outstretched. "Why don't we have a seat in the living room and you can tell me to what do we owe this pleasure?" Meredith led the way, Dad followed, and I slunk in behind them.

Once we were all seated in the living room–Dad and Meredith on the couch–I huddled in the recliner, Dad turned to Meredith. "So, what exactly are you doing here? Is there something wrong with the campaign we discussed?"

Okay, so maybe Dad's nervousness was coming from the fact that he thought this woman was unhappy with his work. I still thought it was pretty damn odd that someone would just show up on our doorstep instead of calling to set up another meeting.

"Actually, after you left, the partners and I discussed your campaign and we absolutely love it. So much, in fact, that we want to ask you to head up another campaign for a sub-company of ours. That's why I'm here. I was so excited to tell you the good news that I thought I'd just follow you back from Masen and deliver it in person," Meredith explained. "I have a friend in the area that I'll be staying with, and I thought we could get together for lunch tomorrow to discuss the details."

She had such an excited buzz about her and her smile was about to drive me nuts, so I took her story for what it was. Dad took a deep breath and visibly relaxed. "Well, that is fantastic news. I'd be honored to head up another campaign for you. And yes, lunch tomorrow sounds great. " Dad grinned and looked in my direction. His smile faltered slightly as he took in my expression. I was sure I wasn't sporting the most gracious look on my face. Whether I believed her story or not, for some reason I just didn't like this woman very much. Maybe it was because she looked so much like my mom.

CHAPTER TWENTY

Old Friend

(Evie)

After Dax and I had settled on the questions that I needed to ask my Sire, I had requested to be left alone. I couldn't remember the last time I had spoken to Balam. It had been so long ago that I had been triggered and made a Sire that it truly felt like a completely different lifetime. Even though I considered my Sire an old friend, I was still a bit nervous to actually be contacting him.

Usually once a new Sire left their original clan to begin their own, there was no further contact between them. Not that it was forbidden, but it was usually just not a necessity, and for whatever ancient reason, that's just how things worked.

Traditionally, once a vampire was confirmed as the triggered vampire in their current clan, they were then led through history lessons about their kind. This included all the different new "powers" that came with being a Sire: the poison of true death, the sedative of eternal life, the scanning abilities, and the importance of choosing their consort. Once they received the guidelines on how to use each of these things, they would then go through the "Passing of Powers" ritual. This is where their Sire passed abilities onto them. They were then expected to leave their current clan, set up a new home location, and begin building a clan/family of their own.

The first vampire that they sired became their consort and shared in their scanning abilities. This was the most important, and the first thing a new Sire needed to do. They had to choose wisely, because once their consort was changed, they were eternally bound to them and if they died...so did the new Sire.

After choosing their consort, there was no limit to how many vampires they could create. The process of the change was pretty typical. The Sire bit the chosen person, and then injected them with the sedative of eternal life. The sire would then feed from the person until they were dead. Once the new vampire had risen, the first thing they were made to do was drink from the Sire. That sealed the bond and completed the process. Once the bond was made, the new vampire then drifted to their "normal" coloring. Most people rose as light vampires, but like Terrance, if they carried sorrow and pain within them, they would mostly likely show signs of that by drifting to a darker color.

As I sat there recalling all the lessons that Balam had taught me, I started to feel a little more relaxed about contacting the man who had blessed me with eternal life, even though I hadn't spoken to him in over a thousand years.

After digging his number out of my archives, I took a deep

breath and dialed.

"Hola, habla Balam."

I smiled. His accent still carried its Mayan heritage, and even though he could speak English, he chose to speak modern Spanish. To this day he continued to go by his real Mayan name, Balam. Just hearing his voice made me realize how much I'd missed him.

"Hello Balam, this is Evangeline."

"Evangeline mi amor, no te he visto en mucho tiempo"

He knew that I hadn't spoken Spanish for hundreds of years, but he was going to make me ask anyway. "Balam, you know I no longer speak Spanish, may I ask that we speak in English, my Sire?" He was very formal when it came to titles and respect.

His only reaction to my request was a small "hmph," and then he said, "Yes of course my darling. I was just saying it has been forever." His voice was kind and immediately took me back to the villages of Chichen Itza. I wasn't originally from Yucatan, but when I was turned by Balam, who was one of the original Mayan people, Chichen Itza was where the clan had actually lived. I had been amazed when I realized that the lair of a centuries old vampire clan resided below the ruins and still did to this day.

"To what do I owe this pleasure?" Balam asked.

"I have a situation developing within my clan that I have never experienced before, and I need to ask you some questions." I figured there was no point in beating around the bush.

"What's the situation?" Apparently he shared my desire to get straight down to business.

"I have a vampire who has drifted permanently dark, which is unfortunate but not unheard of. The problem I'm having with him, however, is that when I scanned him, trying to reveal the cause of his darkening, I was forced into unconsciousness and trapped there until I cleared my mind of the incident." Balam

continued to listen as I explained further. "It was only then that I

was able to wake. My vampire also reports that whenever he

thinks of a particular woman, his thoughts get...fuzzy." I hoped I

was giving him enough details to explain the oddness of my

situation properly.

Silence lingered for more time than I was comfortable with,

but I knew that I needed to let Balam process this information.

The man had a millennium of experience and history to sort

through. I just hoped that something rang a bell.

"Have any of your other vampires drifted permanently dark,

or is it just this one?" His voice was calm, but serious.

"No. Just Terrance."

"And you say that his thoughts get *fuzzy* when he thinks of a

particular woman, correct?"

"Yes. And I think that due to our mental connection,

whatever this woman has done to Terrance is why I was

knocked out when I tried to scan him."

"Yes, I would suspect that the mental connection with Terrance and the image of this woman is related to why you were knocked unconscious."

It seemed like he had an idea of what was happening, so I was only happy to wait for his next question.

"Has Terrance shown any aggression towards the other vampires in your clan?"

"No. We have him chained up right now, and he's not exactly happy about it, but he hasn't tried to hurt any of us. Dax and I noticed about six months ago that he started to have trouble drifting back after feeding and he started to become very quiet and solitary. We started keeping an eye on him, making sure he fed with the others, instead of by himself. And up until last week, he had never killed anyone before, but now he appears to have drifted permanently dark." I couldn't help the sadness in my voice. I really didn't want to have to deliver the true death to him.

"Evangeline, even though as the Sire you are immune, it is absolutely imperative that none of your other vampires get close to Terrance from now on. He is a danger to your clan."

"What? Why? He's chained up, and like I said, he hasn't shown any sign of aggression towards any of us." This was starting to confuse and scare me.

"Evangeline, please do as I say. I don't want any of your other vampires to become infected."

"Infected? What are you talking about?" This conversation was definitely not going how I'd imagined.

"Yes. Infected. I'm almost certain that the woman that Terrance encountered was in fact a zôt—or what you would refer to as a demon."

* * * * *

CHAPTER TWENTY-ONE

Lunch with Barbie

(Rose)

I watched Meredith scoot closer and closer to Dad as they made plans to meet for lunch the following day. I had found a creative form of entertainment that allowed me to remain calm throughout the rest of her unexpected visit. I repeatedly imagined myself flying across the room and strangling her to death to pass the time. It was pretty fun.

Once she had finally left I excused myself and headed straight to my room. I thought it would be best to avoid any conversations about her at that moment. You know the saying...if you can't say anything nice, don't say anything at all.

A few minutes later Dad knocked on my door. "Honey, are you alright?"

"I'm fine, Dad. I just want to go to sleep." I could tell he was considering pressing the issue, but thank god, he didn't.

"Okay, honey. Goodnight then. Oh, and Rose, I'd like you to go with me tomorrow. Meredith and I are meeting at the café in the business district for lunch, and I thought you could do some shopping while I met with her. Then we could take in a movie or something." Dad sounded so upbeat, and after our argument tonight I really did want the chance to continue our conversation about getting a car and moving out.

"Okay Dad, sure thing. That sounds just great." I would fake it for him, but I still didn't like the fact that my dad was going to be having lunch with Barbie.

* * * * *

(Jeremy/Dad)

That had been quite a surprise. I couldn't believe Meredith

had followed me back from Masen, straight to my house no less.

I had told her when we started to see each other every month

during my overnight visits to Masen that she was going to have

to understand that there was no way that I could bring her here

to the house where Rose's mother had been killed, especially

since she looked so much like her.

It was over a year ago that I had met Meredith, and even

then, it had been a shock to me that she looked so much like my

wife. If I was being honest with myself, the fact that she did

resemble Loraine so much had probably contributed to why I

had gravitated to her to begin with. But once we began to spend

some quality time together, I realized that she was a wonderful

person and the fact that she furthered my career had nothing to do with it.

I didn't know how I was going to tell Rose that Meredith and I had been seeing each other, so for now, I thought lunch and some casual conversation would be the perfect place to start.

* * * * *

(Rose)

After Dad and I made breakfast, we went online to search for what he thought would be a dependable brand of car for me. We figured we would narrow down our choices today, and when the car lots opened tomorrow, we wouldn't have to waste much time running around from place to place.

"I really like the Ford Focus," Dad said for the hundredth time.

"I don't mind that one I guess. Though the new Mercedes

look hot," I giggled. I had never been a car person, so the fact that I even knew the name of a certain kind was pretty much a joke. I also had never really been into name brands, so as far as I was concerned, it really didn't matter to me what I got as long as I got one that I could call my own.

It was about 11 a.m. when we shut the computer off and started to get ready. I wasn't exactly sure why Dad wanted me to go. I mean, I was all up for some shopping, but I really wasn't looking forward to seeing Meredith again. The fact that she looked so much like Mom totally creeped me out.

At 12:30 p.m., Dad's voice echoed up the stairs. "Rose? You ready to go?"

"Yep. Be right down." As I rounded the bottom of the stairs and caught a glimpse at what Dad was wearing, I had to hold back a snicker. I had expected him to be dressed in his usual business suit or his Sunday best. But instead, he was dressed in a nice pair of stylish jeans, a white button up shirt that he had left untucked, and his leather jacket that I hadn't seen in

ages. He had also left a slight five o'clock shadow on his face. I

guess he was trying to go for that scruffy, sexy older man look.

But, oh my God, this was my dad. What the hell was he

thinking? And all of a sudden, it dawned on me. Meredith was

more than just a client. And now it looked like I truly would

have to kill her.

* * * * *

CHAPTER TWENTY-TWO

History Lesson

(Evie)

After hearing Balam's idea about what had happened to
Terrance, I had sat there in complete shock. I had no idea what
to say or what to think. I had never believed in demons or
whatever he had called them–zôts. So after allowing me a few
moments to calm myself, he continued, trying to explain.

The history lesson that I received went back thousands of
years, to the time when the Mayan people were facing the threat
of extinction. He explained that Yum Camil, the demon ruler in
Xibalba, had sent forth his favored son, Camazotz, the demon
bat-god, or blood-feeder, into the human realm. He had told him

that he needed to bite and infect as many humans as possible

before the end, so that their bloodline would continue on.

Because even as demons, they weren't going to escape the end

that was quickly approaching their civilization.

Camazotz went into the world at his father's request. He bit

and infected as many people as he could, transforming humans

into zôts. Demons that fed on blood. And this was the

beginning of the vampire race.

I couldn't wrap my head around the fact that Balam was one

of the direct descendants of the first vampires ever created.

Though Yum Camil and Camazotz were classified as

demons, they weren't inherently evil, so when Camazotz infected

the humans, it was the combination of his blood and the light

within the human soul that manifested into the ability of drifting.

Balam continued to explain that after some time, the

vampires that Camazotz was creating started having a bad

reaction to the change.

Balam's theory was that Camazotz, in his effort to complete

his father's mission, remained in the human realm for too long.

Being out of his natural environment for such an extended

period of time had caused his blood to become contaminated.

Camazotz's contaminated blood had infected the new

vampires, and right from the start they had drifted straight to

dark. Soon after, they became violent and turned on their clan.

Once the fighting began, it became obvious that the dark

vampires were passing their infection to the others. Because

when a light vampire was bit, they too, drifted dark.

Soon the dark vampires started to outnumber the light ones,

and the originals feared that they were going to be overrun.

Camazotz then called upon his father to come aid him in

what could only be described as a civil war amongst vampires.

Yum Camil came to his son's aid and found that the only way to

kill the darkened vampires was for him to bite them again,

infecting them with a poison that only he, the ruler of Xibalba, possessed. Upon realizing this, Yum Camil chose a few light vampires, and through his Mayan magic, blessed each of them with the ability to reproduce his poison. These vampires became the first Sires who possessed the poison of true death.

After sending Camazotz back to Xibalba, Yum Camil and the newly created Sires fought to destroy all the darkened vampires. Once the dark ones were eliminated, Yum Camil conducted the first "Passing of Powers" ritual.

In order to bestow the Sires with the sedative of eternal life that was needed to create new vampires, he had to link minds with them. Linking minds with Yum Camil is what led the Sires to have the ability to scan. During this initial rite he also bestowed a time-limit on how long the Sires could hold their powers. This was to prevent a Sire's blood from becoming contaminated like Camazotz's had. He then taught the Sires how to perform the "Passing of Powers" ritual, and then decreed that the Sires divide the remaining light ones into clans and separate to the four corners of the world.

I thought this was where the lesson would stop, but Balam continued to explain the one key point that was relevant to my current situation.

He explained that once the Sires had separated, before returning to Xibalba, Yum Camil continued to infect humans with his *own* blood. Since he wasn't a blood-feeder by nature like his son the Bat God, the humans weren't transformed into vampires. Instead, they remained human, but had demon blood flowing through their veins. It was this line of humans that had continued to exist throughout time, hiding their demon heritage from the world.

This was the only way that Yum Camil could guarantee that his bloodline would continue, since the humans his son had bitten ended up as a new species entirely. That had been an unforeseen twist to his plan. Balam had explained that Yum Camil hadn't meant for the humans he infected to be a threat to anyone, but that like any dying God, only wanted to meet his end knowing that some part of his race would live on. Obviously he had not taken into account how the two species, his demons and his son's vampires would interact. Who would have ever guessed that they would be like poison to one another?

Apparently the woman Terrance bit six months ago was one of the demon descendants of Yum Camil. Her demon blood had infected him and was the reason behind his fuzzy thoughts and his now permanent darkness.

It was more important than ever to find out just who this woman was. And since the infection prevented me or Terrance from accessing any further information about her, I had no idea how we were going to do that.

Before ending our conversation, I had asked Balam if there was any hope of saving Terrance. His answer had been just what I expected: not that he knew of. Dax was not going to be happy about all I had learned. And right now, I couldn't imagine facing all of them with this kind of news. How was I supposed to explain that all of our lives had just changed and that we were now being faced with demons?

Our feedings were going to have to become very strict and limited to only people we'd fed from before. Because now that it was clear that at least one family with demon blood resided in our area, who knew how many more could be out there? I just couldn't take the risk of any other member of my clan becoming infected.

By the time I finished my phone call, the club was in full swing. I found Dax talking to one of the members of the liquor board who had apparently stopped in to make an impromptu inspection. They seemed to be going through the checklist that the inspector was carrying with him. As the owner, I should have made an appearance and schmoozed the pencil pusher like I always did, but after everything that had happened, I just didn't have the energy to deal with that tonight.

Just as I slid back inside my office, Christian appeared in the doorway.

"Evie, are you alright?" he asked.

I could tell he was nervous, and like the rest of them, probably wanting to know what I had learned. But with Dax and the rest of the clan occupied with their jobs, it was the perfect opportunity to have a conversation with Christian about his potential triggering. "I'm fine Christian, but please come in."

* * * * *

CHAPTER TWENTY-THREE

Business Acquaintance

(Rose)

As we drove to the café, I just couldn't bring myself to

question Dad about his relationship with Meredith. So instead, I

sat there imagining all the expensive things I was going to buy

with the credit card he'd given me, while he pretended to have a

business meeting with his whore. Yes, I was that mad.

How in the hell could Dad continue to tell me that it was

"too soon" to move on, when he apparently didn't have any

trouble moving on from Mom's death whatsoever? The more

and more I thought about this, the angrier I was becoming. The

rage inside of me was building at a steady pace, and I felt the tears threatening to spill.

"So, like I said, I figured you could do some shopping while Meredith and I have our meeting. I think I remember you mentioning that you needed some supplies for school and some new cookware to replace the things that I ruined at the house," Dad said with a chuckle. "I'll text you once we're done, and then you and I can go to see that new movie that came out. Sound good?"

I can't tell you how hard it was not to scream at him. It took everything I had to say, "Sure Dad. That'll be fine." I had to keep my head turned towards the window, because if I actually looked at him, I knew I would break. But apparently, diverting my face wasn't enough to hide the waves of tension that were rolling off of me.

"Is something wrong Rose?" he asked.

Damn it, why couldn't he have just let it drop? "Well, Dad, now that you mention it, I guess I'm not really looking forward to seeing Meredith again, since it's obvious that she is more to you than just a *business acquaintance*." I knew my voice carried a tinge of anger, and I didn't care.

A sigh escaped his lips, as he shook his head back and forth. "Rose, I'm so sorry. I had no intention of dating Meredith when we first met, but after getting to know her, we really hit it off, and spending time with her has truly helped me deal with my grief. I didn't say anything because I just didn't think you would understand." Guilt as thick as molasses dripped from his voice.

"Oh no Dad, I understand just fine. You banging someone that looks just like Mom really helps lessen the blow that she's truly gone." Fuck being nice; I'd had enough of being kept in the dark.

"Rose Reynolds! You watch your mouth. How dare you say such a thing to me? I loved your mother with all my heart and I would never disrespect her memory by using someone else as a substitute for what we had together. Yes, Meredith does have similar features to your mother's, but what's really important is that she makes me feel alive again, which is something that I never thought would happen. Don't you dare think you are old enough to understand what I've gone through."

I was confused by his last comment, but didn't have time to dwell on it since we had just pulled up to the café. I threw open the door and bolted from car, "Enjoy your lunch Dad. *Maybe* I'll see you at home?" I ran into the crowd before Dad even had a chance to shut off the car. I noticed Meredith sitting at one of the café tables as I ran by. She looked up, preparing to smile, but then got the most curious look on her face. I was extremely angry, and seeing the most vicious frown form on that bitch's face had only made it worse.

(Jeremy/Dad)

"Jeremy, what's happened?" Meredith asked me as I approached the table.

"Rose knows about us, and it didn't go well," I explained.

Damn it. I hadn't wanted her to find out like this. I had hoped to have a successful business meeting with Meredith before things turned personal. I was planning to tell Meredith that I wanted to let Rose know about us, and then ask Rose to join us for dessert. That way they could spend a little time getting to know each other before I shared the news. So much for that plan.

I had never seen Rose act that way. She had always been so level-headed, and such a good girl. I couldn't believe the venom that her words had carried.

"I should go after her." I started to panic, because I

suddenly remembered the last words Rose had said, *"Maybe I'll*

see you at home." I had to find her before she did something

stupid.

"Jeremy, I think you should just let her blow off some

steam. She'll cool down after a while and then we can go look

for her. The fact that she doesn't have a car yet is definitely a

good thing right now. She shouldn't be able to get too far,"

Meredith reasoned.

"I guess you're right." Resolved to let Rose cool down

before we continued this *conversation*, I sat down and reached for

Meredith's hand. "Thank you. I'm really glad that you're here."

* * * * *

(Rose)

Watching Dad reach for that bitch's hand made me want to scream. I had run into the nearest alley between two of the shops and propped myself up against the brick wall while I tried to catch my breath. Then I had peeked out to see how close behind me Dad was. But, to my surprise, he wasn't even following me. He had sat down with Meredith instead and then reached for her hand.

That was it. I'd had it. I had been feeling guilty that I was going to be moving out and leaving Dad all alone, but it was pretty fucking obvious that he had someone else to fill the void that Mom, and now I, would be leaving in his life. What a bastard.

* * * * *

CHAPTER TWENTY-FOUR

Dream Come True

(Christian)

As I entered Evie's office, I could tell that whatever she had
learned from her Sire had left her shaken. Her hair had drifted a
little darker and it looked like she had run her fingers through it
a number of times. But I just couldn't control my curiosity.
"What did you find out from Balam?"

After she lowered herself into her chair, she closed her eyes,
and took a deep breath. "I think it's best if I tell everyone the
information I learned from Balam after closing, but right now
there is something else that I want to discuss with you."

Damn, I really wanted to get to the bottom of this, and

waiting until closing to find out what Evie had learned was going to be torture. "Okay, what is it?"

"Well, I'll cut right to the chase. I have reasons to believe that you are being triggered to become the new Sire." Even though she looked tired, the smile on her face indicated that for her, this was good news.

"Are you kidding me?" I was starting to feel a little anxious, since this was the second time that someone had mentioned this to me.

"No, Christian. I'm not kidding you. And if I'm right, it will be a dream come true for me. From the moment that I found you on the Swedish island of Gotland, it was clear to me that you were a wonderful person." She paused, reflecting briefly. "It was actually a coincidence that Dax and I even stopped on your island. I remember that we were travelling through the Baltic Sea and there was a problem with the ship. Once it docked, we decided it would be best if we explored the island to feed, rather than remain with the boat." She looked at me with such pride in her eyes. "It was the best decision that we ever made."

Evie rose from her chair and continued to relive the story that brought her and Dax to find me. "I remember stumbling upon your little village and seeing all the hardworking people, and the sense of community. As we watched from afar, I told Dax that I only wanted to have a small clan so that we would always remain as close as the people we saw there."

"I've always wondered why you created so few vampires for your clan." I had never asked, mainly because I thought it would be rude, but apparently she had gotten her wish. Our small clan had always been happy...until now.

"We watched your village for several days and fed only when someone would head to the stream for water. Dax had dug out a burrow that provided us safety while we slept, but then one day, we awoke to screams."

I knew the day she was referring to; it was the last and first day of my life.

"The crew of the boat had discovered your village. When we reached them, they had already started to plunder and pillage. I remember seeing you fighting so fiercely to protect that young girl. Dax and I fought off everyone we could while trying to not frighten your townsfolk, but by the time we reached you, you had been stabbed through." Evie had circled behind me and now rested her hands on my shoulders. "There was no way I could let you die. Not after seeing what a wonderful person you were. So helpful to your village, such a hard worker, and an amazing fighter. I knew in that instant that you would become my son. My first vampire son."

Evie squeezed my shoulders and then made her way back around to sit behind her desk once more. "If you are in fact the one being triggered, I want you to know that I couldn't be happier or prouder."

I sat stunned for a moment. Not because of her speech, but

because I hadn't thought of that day in so long. It was going to take me a minute to shake the memories from my head. "I'm at a loss for words. Honestly, I feel like there has to be some mistake. I haven't shown any signs of being triggered and..." My words drifted off as I truly didn't know what to say.

"Actually, you have been showing signs. Remember in the private room when I launched myself at you? It was because you had commented on something that I had *thought*–not said. I was so shocked and surprised that I literally flew across the room to see if I had imagined things. But then we were interrupted and I couldn't explain."

As I sat there dumbfounded, she continued, "Then there's the fact that when I was trapped in the comatose state, you just happened to *know* what the right thing to do was. I actually think that's because you are developing the psychic ability called claircognizance, which means 'clear knowing'. Then, when you were outside the office tonight, you had the most quizzical look on your face so I scanned you and found that you had heard Dax and my conversation by accident. I can honestly say that I have never experienced any of these things myself, but it leads me to believe that you are in fact the one being triggered." Evie sat there just looking at me with a smile on her face.

I couldn't move. I sat there stunned then had to shake my head in order to knock my brain back into gear. "I just thought my hearing had been doing weird things. I have heard some people whisper a couple things, and then accidentally honed-in on your and Dax's conversation. And as far as the "knowing"— I'm not sure how I knew how to help you when you were comatose. But really Evie, I don't see how that can equal me being triggered. I thought there were *specific* signs to look for." I was confused and a little nauseous. I just couldn't wrap my head around this. I couldn't possibly be the one.

"I have been wondering that too, so when I spoke to Balam, I asked him if all Sires show the same symptoms when they are triggered. He informed me that each Sire is different. It's the fact that you are starting to display *any* new powers that identifies you as the one being triggered. Now, as to what those powers might be, that's something that is individual to each vampire. The scanning ability, the sedative of eternal life, and the poison of true death are all things that are passed between Sires during the Passing of Powers ritual, but each Sire usually has an additional power or two that they develop during their triggering. When I was triggered, I actually developed the ability of telekinesis. I could move objects with my mind." Evie demonstrated by moving a stapler from one side of her desk to the other. "It is not something that I use very often, and it's also something that only Dax and Balam know about."

I must have looked comical to Evie because I was sitting there with my mouth gaping open and my eyes bugging out of my head. I couldn't believe the shit that was happening lately. No way could I be the next Sire. And I couldn't believe that she had never told us that she could move shit with her mind! I also couldn't believe the amount of information and history that was being kept just between the Sires. Now I was really curious as to what other secrets Evie would be sharing with us later tonight.

"Christian, are you okay?"

When I finally looked up and met Evie's eyes, I could tell that she was worried about me. And honestly, I didn't know if I was okay or not. This was just so much to process and we hadn't even gotten to the situation with Terrance yet. I just wasn't sure if I could deal with this right now, and truth be told, I wasn't sure I wanted to become the next Sire. The one thing that I did know about becoming a Sire was that it meant I would have to leave the only family I had known for over 600 years. I couldn't imagine leaving my family or Rose. *Wait...Rose.* If I became the new Sire, I would be able to change Rose! No petitioning, no waiting, I would be able to change her and then we could truly be together forever.

"Evie, if I am the one who's been triggered to become the next Sire, can you tell me how the consort bond works?" I couldn't hold back the excitement in my voice. This suddenly had the potential to become very good news.

"I know what you're thinking Christian, and yes, you would be able to choose Rose as your consort. But, that is a very important decision and one that isn't without consequences."

Just as I was about to push the subject, Dax opened the door and strolled inside to take the seat next to me. "Liquor board inspection is done. We're good." He looked between the two of us, and probably noticed that I was on the edge of my chair and Evie was leaning forward with her forearms resting on her desk. "Everything okay? You guys look a little tense."

"Everything is fine. I was just explaining to Christian that I believe that he is the one being triggered to become the new Sire." Evie looked at him with a firm set to her chin.

Dax pushed out of the chair and started pacing. "Dammit,

Evie! I thought we agreed to not bring this up until everything was settled with Terrance."

"If you recall my dear, I didn't agree to anything. I know you expressed that you thought it was for the best, but I never agreed to remain quiet. Plus, after what I have learned from Balam, I think it's necessary for Christian to understand what is happening to him. He may actually be of great use to us in figuring out what's happening with Terrance."

Great. This sounded ominous, and not something I really wanted to be involved in. Like I had said, Terrance was an asshole and I didn't want to have anything else to do with him.

Dax sighed, and the look he gave Evie wasn't exactly a loving one, but then he said, "Okay Evie. Whatever you think is best." He then quietly left the room, closing the door behind him.

"Why do you think I'll be able to help figure out what's going on with Terrance?" I really didn't want to know, but I thought it would be best if I knew exactly what Evie was expecting of me.

"I'm not sure yet, but I feel that if we can keep tabs on your developing powers, especially the claircognizance, it might be of use in the situation." Evie rose from her chair and I followed suit. She hugged me then held my shoulders tight as she looked into my eyes. "Everything will work out Christian, you'll see. Just please come to me if you experience any strange sensations or if you have questions about what's happening to you. Again, I can't tell you how proud I am of you."

As I headed for the door, I looked back at Evie and forced a smile onto my face. I wanted her to know that her pride in me was definitely something I appreciated, but I was sure that my smile only came off as fake. I didn't share her sentiment that everything would work out. As a matter of fact, whether it was my new found *psychic ability* or not, I suddenly felt that things were going to get a lot worse.

* * * * *

CHAPTER TWENTY-FIVE

Head East

(Rose)

I couldn't stand to watch my dad sit there with that bitch for a second longer. Now that it was obvious there would be no shopping and no movie in my near future, I pulled out my cell phone and dialed Jillian. "Hey can you please come pick me up at the northwest corner of the business district? I have to get the fuck out of here NOW!"

Jillian started to question me about what was wrong, but I just didn't have the patience to explain it to her over the phone. After grasping my level of frustration she agreed to come pick me up right away.

"I can't believe your dad is actually seeing someone and didn't even tell you about it." Her shock was genuine, but I was too mad to discuss it.

"Can we just not talk about it?" I asked. "I would love it if we could just go for a drive. I'll pay for the gas. I just need some time to get rid of this angry feeling before I can process any of this."

"You got it. Where do you wanna go?"

"I don't care. Let's just head east I guess." I really didn't have a specific destination in mind, but it was beautiful this time of year, and the idea of taking in a little of the countryside sounded just about perfect right now.

Jillian hummed along to the radio as we drove and I stared out the window watching the trees go by. I kept thinking about all those overnight trips that Dad had made to Masen. It was pretty damn obvious that he had spent them with her, and I couldn't help but wonder how long it had been going on. It still pissed me off to think that he had just jumped into a relationship

right after Mom had died, and I still didn't understand the

statement he had made about me not knowing everything he'd

gone through. What the hell was that supposed to mean anyway?

I was lost in my thoughts as I tried to process everything

that had happened since Meredith's visit: the way she had

scooted closer to Dad on the couch, seeing him in that

ridiculous "hip" outfit that was obviously meant to impress her,

and then watching her comfort him at the café. But what had

really struck me as odd, was the strange, almost angry look that

Meredith had given me as I ran by her table today.

I could understand that I probably looked a bit distressed,

but then wouldn't you think that she would have had a surprised

or concerned look on her face instead of an angry one? What the

fuck did she have to be angry at me about? She was the one who

was secretly sleeping with my dad, so if anyone had the right to

be angry, it was me! This line of thinking wasn't helping me calm down, instead I was starting to get even more pissed off, but then a bump in the road jostled my attention back to the present.

"Hey, where are we?" I asked Jillian. I didn't recognize the road we were now traveling down.

"I turned off the highway a little ways back. It's almost dark and this is the town Justin is from. I thought that since we were this close, I'd drive through and check it out."

Jillian's answer surprised me. I had forgotten all about her new vampire boyfriend. Of course it hadn't surprised me that he'd made some sort of excuse to be unavailable until after dark.

Thinking about Justin pulled my thoughts back to my incident at the apartment complex. After having my melt down at that pool, all the images from my first encounter with a vampire had started to replay in my head.

It had been only about seven and a half months ago, right after I had started seeing Christian, when I had made plans with Mom to stay late after school in order to get some research done in the library. She was supposed to come pick me up after her swim lesson was over, but instead, she had called saying that her lesson was going to run late and that I should take the bus to meet her. She had given me the address of the training facility, and by the time I arrived, it was just barely after dark.

As I approached the pool, I didn't hear anything, but instead saw thrashing waves in the pool. Once I looked closer, I saw my mom and a guy struggling underwater. Instead of throwing my bags to the ground and diving in like I should have, I completely froze. I couldn't move or scream, and after a moment the waves in the water started to clear. What I saw was enough to scare me into hiding. I ran back around the corner of the building and watched as the man climbed out of the pool carrying my mother in his arms with his mouth plastered to the side of her neck.

At first, I had thought, "Holy shit, my mom is having an affair," but once I looked closer I could tell that he wasn't kissing the side of her neck. He had sharp teeth that appeared to be piercing her instead. I quickly realized that what I had first

thought were sensual kisses were actually long drags of sucking.

This man was drinking from my mother.

I had sunk to the ground not knowing what to do or think.

I remembered feeling like I was going to pass out. But as I

continued to watch, the man finally removed what could only be

called fangs from my mom's neck. He then laid her on one of

the chaise lounges next to the pool and gently brushed the hair

out of her eyes. She sat up with a smile on her face and waved as

the man started to walk away. I was so relieved to see that she

was okay that I sucked in a quick breath. The man's head spun in

my direction and he stared me down with intense, dark eyes.

After a moment, he crooked his finger at me, indicating for

me to come to him. I was still frozen in fear and literally couldn't

move. The next thing I knew he was standing right in front of

me. Only a split-second had passed and I hadn't even seen him

move, but there he was, dripping wet, towering over me with a cocky smirk on his face.

"Hi. You must be the daughter." His voice was deep and
sexy, just like the rest of him. I couldn't believe that I had had
those thoughts about a man who had just been holding my
mother so intimately, but I couldn't deny reality. The guy
appeared to be in his mid-thirties, with dark brown hair and eyes
to match. He was tan and muscular, and probably about 6' 4".
He looked like sex-on-a-stick.

"Yes, I'm her daughter. Who the hell are you?" I had finally
gotten myself under control and stood up to face him.

"I think the question you want to ask is 'What are you?', am
I right?" He had a mocking glint in his eye, and that damn cocky
grin was still plastered to his face.

"I'm not stupid. I know what you are." Whether I wanted to
believe it or not, it was obvious that this *man* was..."You're a
vampire."

His grin widened. "Are you scared?"

"Should I be?" I tried to bolster myself so that the fear I was feeling wouldn't come across in my shaking voice.

He stared at me for a long time then gave a slight *hmph*. "No, beautiful, you have nothing to fear from me. One a night is all I can handle."

I hated that his *one* had been my mom, but I was damn glad that he would be leaving me alone. "Did you hurt her?" Now that I felt somewhat safe, I had a shit-ton of questions that I was dying to ask him. Well, maybe dying wasn't the right word to use.

"No, I didn't hurt her, and she won't remember anything about tonight," he explained. "What about you? Should I bite you and make you forget?" He seemed genuine in his question.

I tried not to shiver, and the goose bumps his question produced spread up my arms. "No. I don't want to forget. Actually, I have a lot of questions that I would love to ask you. I'm a history major and I can't tell you what an amazing paper I could write with your help." Seriously. I had just asked a vampire to help me get a good grade on my history paper.

He turned around and saw that my mom had gotten up from her chaise and was starting to gather her things. "Why don't you meet me back here tomorrow night and I'll answer some of your questions."

"Really? Or is this some kind of trick to get me here so I can be the one you feed from tomorrow?" I was excited but not stupid. I wondered if crosses or stakes would actually work on this guy. Not that I'm Buffy, but a girl could try.

"No trick. I do, however, enjoy the taste of your mother's blood. It's different than any other that I've ever experienced. So once you spend the evening with her and realize that I'm telling the truth and that I didn't hurt her in any way, as long as I can continue to feed from your mom...I'll be willing to answer your questions. Is that something that you can handle?" He extended his hand as if preparing to shake on a deal.

"Okay. But if Mom shows any signs of being hurt or acting weird, then you'll never see us here again." It was a lame threat because he could probably just follow us home or find us whenever he wanted, but I had to make sure he understood that if he had hurt my mom in any way, the deal was off.

"Deal." He shook my hand and then started to walk away. "Oh. One more thing. What's your name?"

"My name is Rose. What's yours?"

"Terrance. My name is Terrance."

CHAPTER TWENTY-SIX

Bad Night

(Christian)

After we finished closing the club, we all gathered around

waiting for Evie to share what she had learned from Balam.

"What I have to tell you is going to come as quite a shock,"

she stated. "I'm not going to recount the entire history of the

how's or why's, but what we've come to figure out is that a

woman that Terrance fed from, the woman I saw in his

thoughts, is a zôt—or what you would call a demon."

Gasps and curses filled the room. Dax collapsed into a chair

and Evie placed a hand on his shoulder. "The zôt's blood is the

reason behind his odd behavior. It acts like a poison and literally infects him. It's what is causing his memory loss and his thoughts to become fuzzy whenever he tries to think of her. Apparently the demon's blood has something like a built-in protection feature. It is how they have kept themselves hidden throughout history. It's also what is causing him to drift permanently dark." The sadness in her voice was the first indication that this was going to be a bad night.

"So, if this is an infection, is there any way to cure him?" Bobby asked.

"No, honey. Not that we know of." Evie's eyes filled with tears as she took a seat next to Dax.

"Okay. If this woman is a zôt, or demon, or what-the-fuck-ever, but we can't figure out who she is because of the automatic brain-fuck her blood causes, then how the hell are we supposed to find her? I, for one, do not want to accidentally feed on some fucking demon." Tori's hair was drifting from light red to a seriously deep maroon color. She was pissed and had never been one to hold back her feelings.

"Until we get to the bottom of this, I think it's for the best if we only feed from people that we have previously fed from before since we know them to already be safe. I'm thinking that throughout the night we can each take a turn and invite a previous guest to one of the private rooms. This way we can remain safe inside the club and not risk running across another zôt while hunting outside. Just make sure that when you feed from them you use your sedative to get them to come back again and again." She didn't look happy about this idea, but continued anyway. "Also...no one is to go near Terrance from now on. Apparently, once an infected vampire permanently drifts dark, they can infect other vampires." She looked at me with a look on her face that could only be described as disheartened.

"I have faith that we will get to the bottom of this, but until we do, I'm not going to deliver the true death to Terrance. I want him around in case we find the woman. Maybe by some miracle, locating her can provide the answers we need, or perhaps even a cure we don't yet know about." She stood and with the command in her voice said once again, "No one is to go near Terrance from now on." Evie wasn't stupid and I'm sure she realized that we all planned to interrogate Terrance the first chance we got.

She must have been scanning us because the next thing she said was, "I am going to be questioning Terrance again, and explaining what we've learned. All of you are more than welcome to witness this."

As Evie and Dax headed towards her office, the rest of us just sat there in silence. Finally Dom broke the tension. "Have any of you ever heard of anything like this? Of demons actually existing?"

"No. But I guess it shouldn't come as a huge surprise. I mean, who'd believe that vampires really existed either?" Bobby asked.

He was being way more relaxed about this than I was. I wish I could ask Evie some more questions, but figured we had better head down so we didn't miss her questioning Terrance again. "Come on. Let's get below and see what Terrance has to say about all this." I hit the switch to unlock the stage.

Once we were all downstairs and gathered outside of Terrance's cell, Evie stepped up to the opening and stopped. Obviously she was serious about not getting close to him. "Terrance, I have some news as to what's happened to you."

"Oh, goody. Please then, share with the class." He was being sarcastic and had an almost menacing look on his face.

"You've been infected by demon blood." Evie's statement dropped like a bomb.

Terrance just looked at her, huffed, and shook his head. "Wow, is that the best you can do? I know you want to have a clear conscience when you deliver the true death, but making up bullshit reasons as to why you *have* to kill me is pretty fucking lame."

"Why is he acting like that?" Tori whispered.

Evie turned around and said in a low voice, "I think it has to do with the poison. It literally makes him act dark and then wipes the memories of it from him."

Turning around she continued, "First of all, I don't have to justify delivering the true death to you at all. You've drifted permanently dark, and you know that is grounds for immediate execution. Secondly, I wanted you to know what has happened to you, so that you would understand why you are having trouble remembering things and why your thoughts become fuzzy when you think of that woman. It's her that is the demon. She's the one who has infected you."

Terrance sat there with an angry look on his face. I didn't think he was buying what Evie was trying to explain to him, but then suddenly the lines on his face smoothed out and his eyes seemed to lighten just slightly. "Are you telling me that I'm infected with demon blood for real?"

"Yes, my friend. That is exactly what I'm telling you. We are hoping that once we find her she can provide a cure." Evie's voice carried the hope that we were all feeling.

"Oh, thank God. I just couldn't understand why I had lost it, but I guess now it all makes sense. I never even knew that demons really existed. How in the hell did I run across one?" Terrance seemed to almost be back to his old self, except that his hair remained completely black.

As Evie started to move into the cell, obviously feeling confident in Terrance's breakthrough, I suddenly got the sense that something was terribly wrong. I sprung into the cell, grabbing Evie just as Terrance lunged for her, pulling his chains tight. His eyes were again completely black to match his hair, and his lips were pulled back revealing his fangs as he growled at us.

Dax was up in a flash and carrying Evie out of the cell. "Son of a bitch, Evie. What the fuck were you doing? You're the one who said to stay away from him, and now we know why. He's lost it. He almost bit you."

"It's okay. I know what I'm doing." Evie wiggled free of Dax's arms. She took a moment to glance at everyone. "That, my dears, was a test. And you're right, Terrance has lost it. I wanted you to see why it's so important to stay away from him. He's completely lost to us, and will try to manipulate anyone he gets close to from now on. But I am immune from his bite. I am the only one with the poison of true death, and because of that I can't be infected."

We all stood there completely stunned. "You could have warned me." Dax said.

"No, I couldn't have. I wasn't sure it was going to work." Evie had a timid smile on her face and shrugged her shoulders. Sometimes it was hard to remember that she was over twelve hundred years old.

We all turned and stared at Terrance, who was still baring

his fangs and snapping at us. I couldn't believe how quickly he had deteriorated.

"I hope we can quickly figure out who this woman is. I can't stand to see him like this," Dax said. The sad note in his voice mirrored the look on his face. He hung his head and started to walk off. "I'm going to bed."

Everyone else said their goodnights and headed towards their respective rooms until it was just Evie and myself standing outside the cell. "It happened again didn't it? You *knew* something bad was going to happen when I entered the cell, didn't you?" Evie prodded as we started down the hall.

I guess I couldn't deny it any longer. "Yes. I got an overwhelming sense that something was wrong. But I just can't believe that I'm supposed to become your successor. It's completely unreal to me."

"It could have been anybody in the clan, but I'm glad it's you Christian. You're going to make a wonderful Sire." Evie hugged me.

"How am I supposed to use any of these new skills to help figure out who this woman is? It's not like I can control it." I was feeling so unsure of myself and the things that were apparently now happening as part of my triggering. I had no idea what to do.

"The first thing I would suggest is that when the darkness claims you tonight, let your last thought be of your emerging powers. Concentrate on them and how they make you feel when they happen. Maybe that will trigger something in your subconscious." Evie touched my cheek then headed for her room.

I supposed anything was worth a try. Evie certainly had experience dealing with the subconscious, so maybe she was onto something. Though it was going to be very strange to not have Rose be the last thing I thought of that night, since it had been my ritual for a little over nine months. But just the thought of Rose and the possibility of spending eternity with her was enough motivation to try anything to gain control of my powers. I wanted to be the best Sire and consort to her that I could possibly be.

* * * * *

CHAPTER TWENTY-SEVEN

Hanging Out with Justin

(Rose)

After Jillian explained that this little town was where Justin

was from, I couldn't help but think to myself that if we could

find him this would be the perfect opportunity to see if Justin

could be of any use to me. I had a surprise for Christian—not

only was I going to be moving out, but soon I was also going to

be a vampire just like him so we could be together forever.

I hadn't told Christian that I knew vampires existed yet

because Terrance had warned me that revealing my knowledge

could get us both killed. He also taught me that I had to hide my

thoughts around other vampires, making sure that I only focused on the events that were immediately happening around me. After spending time with him at the pool, I came to learn quite a bit about vampires and how they weren't the bad, evil villains of lore. He had explained that every night they fed from only one person and only took their fill. Using their powers let them make the feeding process an enjoyable act for both vampire and human, and it also allowed them to compel the human so that they didn't remember anything that had happened.

Terrance had continued to feed from my mom and it amazed me how she didn't even care. She never seemed hurt or out of it in any way. There were times when I thought that he may have taken too much blood and that it was going to leave her weak, but she never seemed to show any sign of feeling sick or anemic, so I came to trust Terrance pretty quickly. Once he fed he would use his sedative to put my mom to sleep for a short time so that we could talk.

During our conversations I had told him that initially I had no idea that Christian was a vampire. When we had started

dating, I truly believed that he slept all day because of his job.

Only after meeting Terrance had everything become crystal

clear. After he confirmed that he knew Christian and lived with

him at the club, I had asked him why I had never seen him there

while I visited him. He had explained that it was because he

always left the vicinity to feed, only returning when it was time

for the club to open.

I had continued to see Christian even knowing he was a

vampire, but as I remembered back to the first time I'd seen him

after learning the truth, I recalled how completely nerve-

wracking it had been. I thought for sure it was going to be nearly

impossible to hide my thoughts from Christian, but surprisingly

enough he never seemed to notice a thing. Like I'd said before,

I'd always been pretty good at hiding things from people.

After multiple conversations with Terrance, I had finally

asked the question that I was dying to know. How did someone become a vampire? He explained the process, which really wasn't a surprise. The vampire bit and fed from the human until they drained them, and then the human fed from the vampire in return. They would then die and be reborn as a vampire in a matter of hours. After a few weeks of contemplating it, I had made up my mind that I was definitely in love with Christian and wanted to become like him so that we could be together forever. I asked Terrance if he would be willing to change me and he agreed.

He explained that no one could know that we knew each other or that he was going to change me into a vampire, since this wasn't the usual way that these types of things happened. Apparently the normal way for new vampires to be made was for the clan to vote on who they wanted added to the *family*, but Terrance had agreed to change me in secret because he knew everyone would be happy and understood that I wanted it to be a surprise for Christian.

We had started making plans for my change, but then my mom had died. I had initially thought that Terrance had done it because of the bite marks on her neck, but since he'd only ever fed from my mom at the pool, I ended up quickly coming to the conclusion that it couldn't have been him.

After Mom's death, and once I'd been placed on lockdown by my father, I never saw Terrance again. That is, not until the night he emerged from the woods. It had taken everything I had not to act surprised or let on that I knew him in any way. But since Christian and Evie never mentioned anything, I assumed I had pulled it off. When I saw him, I had wanted so badly to just run and confront him and ask him if he knew what had happened but I'd never had the chance.

Jillian hit the curb as she parked the car, once again shaking me out of my thoughts. "Sorry, I just thought we could grab a bite to eat. I'm starving," she said hesitantly.

"Okay. Yeah, I guess I could eat. Why don't you call Justin

and see if he can come meet us?" I smiled and tried to sound like the supportive friend.

After she phoned Justin and told him that we were in town and invited him to join us, we walked into the restaurant and grabbed a seat by the front windows. Jill kept looking at me over her menu with questions clearly shining in her eyes. "Are you feeling better now?" she finally asked.

"Yes, I am. Thank you for getting me out of town. I just don't think I can deal with my dad right now. He has apparently been seeing this woman, Meredith, and it really took me by surprise. The worst part is that she looks a lot like my mom." I slumped a bit in my chair I just couldn't get over how much that bothered me. I think hanging out with Justin couldn't have come at a better time. I was ready, now more than ever, to leave this world behind. I really hoped he would agree to change me.

As I sat there contemplating how the hell I was going to get Justin alone, the vampire himself came strolling down the sidewalk. I watched him cross the street and head in our

direction. Once Jill saw him, she knocked on the window to gain

his attention. He smiled, waved, and sped towards the front

door.

By the time he reached the table, Jillian was beaming and

Justin only caused her smile to widen as he leaned in to place a

gentle kiss on her lips. "What in the world inspired you two to

head all the way out here?"

"Rose had a mental breakdown and needed to get out of

town." She always did love throwing me under the bus whenever

she could. "I saw the sign for the turnoff and I remembered you

telling me that this was where you were from. Plus, I was getting

hungry."

With a little chuckle he said, "Well that was perfect timing

because I just started getting hungry too."

I almost spit my soda across the table at his obvious

statement. Jill didn't have a clue about him, but it cracked me up to see how many people were mindfucked by the vampires in our area. As the huff left my lungs, I shook my head slightly and looked right at Jill's neck and then back at him. I was trying to be obvious and thought I was getting my message across pretty well because Justin's eyes quickly widened before he squinted and stared right at me.

I nodded and then tilted my head to the side, exposing my neck to him. He smirked and casually licked the tip of one of his fangs. Jillian was completely oblivious. She was actually flagging down the waiter with a huge smile on her face.

Justin turned towards Jillian and took her hand. I thought it was just a sweet gesture until he lifted her wrist to his mouth and bit down. I couldn't believe that he was doing this in the middle of a fucking restaurant, but suddenly he released her hand and I watched as the tiny holes closed immediately, leaving no trace of a puncture behind. Jillian stood up and announced that she needed to use the restroom. It was obvious that he had used his powers to *suggest* that she leave us alone.

Once she was gone, Justin turned towards me. "How do you know about me?" He didn't exactly sound mad, but he definitely sounded concerned.

"I met someone like you who taught me all about vampires. But don't even think about feeding on me or I'll tell Christian and he'll kill you." I wasn't sure I was safe with Justin like I'd been with Terrance, and he didn't know that I hadn't told Christian that I knew his secret yet. Hopefully he wouldn't call my bluff.

"Not that I was planning on feeding on you, but what are you talking about? Christian can't kill me."

"I know that if a human tells anyone they are aware of vampires, it puts them and the vampire at risk of being killed." I wasn't sure why I had to explain this to him, and honestly, I didn't have time for this. There was only one question that I needed to ask him. "I want to know if you'd be willing to change me. I'm completely in love with Christian and I want to surprise him by becoming a vampire so that we can spend eternity together, and the vampire that was going to change me has disappeared."

Justin sat there staring at me like I was completely crazy. I knew that throwing this out there was a bit of a shock but we were going to be out of time soon and I needed an answer. "Well? Will you change me or not?" I demanded.

The severe frown on his face and the slow shake of his head was the first indication that I wasn't going to like his answer. "I don't understand. If a vampire has taught you all about us, then you should know that I *can't* change you. Only a Sire can inflict the change."

I sat there dazed, because I didn't understand what he was saying. Terrance had never mentioned anything about a Sire, or that they were the only ones with the ability to create new vampires. Justin must be using that as an excuse to not change me and that pissed me off. He could have easily just said no.

"Why are you making shit up? You could just tell me no. I could always ask one of the other members of Christian's clan to do it."

"Rose, you don't understand. I'm not making shit up. I'm telling you the truth. Whoever taught you about us has fed you a line of bullshit. Was this person feeding off of you, too?"

"Fuck no. I found him feeding from my mom, and he liked the taste of her blood, so he agreed to teach me about your kind as long as he could continue to feed from her." I was so fucking confused right now, and I couldn't sit still. "Let's get out of here." I flew out of my chair and headed back to the car.

Justin climbed in the driver's seat after depositing Jill in the backseat. He had decided it would be easier for us to talk openly if he used his sedative to knock her out. I gave him the keys and settled into the passenger seat. "Okay, so you're going to have to explain why you think I've been fed a line of bull. My friend has always been honest with me, so I don't understand why he'd lie about that."

"I'm not sure either, but I'll tell you anything you want to know. If some vampire has been manipulating you then there is definitely something seriously wrong. And Rose, I think you need to tell Christian everything."

CHAPTER TWENTY-EIGHT

Serious Problem

(Christian)

The moment I woke from my comatose sleep, I knew there was a serious problem within the clan. But I didn't expect it to be between Terrance and Tori.

Apparently Evie's idea for me to concentrate on my developing powers while I slept had worked, because when I woke the first thing I saw was a vision of Terrance sinking his fangs into Tori's neck.

I headed straight for Terrance's cell expecting the worst, but when I rounded the corner what I saw instead surprised me. Tori was actually walking towards Terrance's cell but she hadn't reached it yet. I guess my vision had been more like a premonition. "Are you okay? What are you doing here?" I asked her.

"I'm going to ask Terrance a few questions of my own." The tone in her voice indicated that she was not happy. "I want to know who this demon bitch is, and I plan to find out even if it takes a bit of *coercion*." The bat she produced from behind her back totally caught me off guard.

I guess she was planning to beat the truth of out Terrance. But thinking back to my "premonition," I knew it wasn't going to work and would end with Terrance's fangs buried in her neck. "Tori, you can't do this. Evie commanded us to stay away from Terrance. I don't even know how you've made it this far, but there's no way I'm letting you put yourself at risk by entering that cell, so just forget it."

Seeing her tiny frame holding that bat was almost comical, but I knew better than to underestimate her. All vampires had preternatural speed and strength, and I knew that if it came to me fighting her off I would win, but I was sure she would put up a damn good fight.

Just as Tori stepped towards me, Evie and Dax turned the corner at the end of the hall. "Tori, stop right there." Evie's command rang in my ears. Tori stopped midstride and remained frozen until Evie reached her.

"I commanded you to stay away from Terrance, so why did you think you'd actually get close enough to him to use that bat?" Evie didn't sound angry, but I could tell it wouldn't take much to push her in that direction.

"When I walked past his cell tonight on my way to Dom's room I noticed that I was able to get really close despite Evie's command. So I went back to my room and grabbed my bat and was just coming back to see if I could make him talk. Someone has to figure out what's going on." Tori's voice was rising and her hair and eyes had begun to drift.

She sounded so upset and I couldn't blame her. I knew she and Terrance had previously been involved, but I think what was really upsetting her had more to do with the fact that she really didn't want to be trapped inside the club, feeding from the same people over and over.

Tori had been raised in a very strict household, and while Dominique had enjoyed the life of a '20s flapper, Tori had been stuck at home, caring for their parents and doing most of the chores. Once their parents had passed away, they had lost their home and Evie found the girls wandering the streets together. Once Tori had awakened from the change, the freedom that came with being a vampire had set her heart to flight. She loved being outside, and I knew that was what she would miss the most.

"Honey, give me the bat. I know you want some answers and obviously think this is a good way to get them, but I promise you...you're wrong. Please don't risk yourself by doing something like this. Terrance will bite you, and then you'll be infected and will drift permanently dark. You know what I'll be forced to do if that happens." Evie held out her hand to take the bat from Tori.

Tori handed Evie the bat, then took a couple steps forward to stare at Terrance as he sat in his cell just glaring at us. "Terrance, can't you tell us anything about this woman? We just want to help you. Please, just tell us." Tori pleaded with him, but I knew it wasn't going to do any good.

He sat there silently just like I knew he would. Evie reached out and placed a hand on Tori's shoulder, and Tori turned and melted into Evie's embrace. As the two women walked off, Dax and I stood outside the cell staring at Terrance.

"Not that I'm ungrateful, but why were you here trying to stop Tori?" Dax asked.

"When I woke this evening, the first thing I saw was an image of Terrance sinking his fangs into Tori's neck." I shrugged my shoulders and started to make my way towards the stairs.

"So, I guess that Evie's right after all. You *are* the one being triggered. How do you feel about that?"

I wasn't sure how I felt about it, and I didn't really know what to say to Dax, but the stress of discussing it was immediately postponed as we reached the top of the stairs. As I emerged from the rising pit, I looked up and found Rose standing in the club...right next to Justin.

* * * * *

CHAPTER TWENTY-NINE

Time for the Truth

(Rose)

After riding around with Justin, I learned that not only had Terrance lied to me, but that I had absolutely no way of becoming a vampire anytime soon. Apparently it was common knowledge between the clans that Evangeline had lost her ability to inflict the change. They were waiting on the next Sire to be triggered, but until then there was no way that I could be made a vampire.

Justin had also informed me that we would not be killed if we told Christian's clan that I was aware that vampires existed. He had explained that the only time a vampire is killed is if they drifted completely dark.

My brain was fuzzy from information overload, but once I had cleared my head I told Justin about Terrance coming out of the woods, Christian's reaction to him, and how he'd had really black hair and dark eyes.

He convinced me to go with him to the club so that we could tell Evangeline about what Terrance had been up to. Since my plan to surprise Christian was ruined and it didn't look like there was going to be a way around it anytime soon, I decided that Justin was right; it was time for the truth.

I was completely petrified about coming clean about what I knew, but for reasons that I couldn't explain, I truly felt that it was the right thing to do.

We arrived at The Rising Pit just before 8 p.m. The door was locked, but Justin knocked once, and Evie opened it with a surprised look on her face and escorted us inside.

"This is a surprise, Rose. I hadn't realized that you knew

Justin. And how in the world did you get away to come visit us on a Sunday night? I know your father is quite strict regarding your schedule."

She was probably wondering if Justin had bit me and brought me to the club so I quickly answered, "Actually Evangeline, Justin brought me here because I have something important that I need to discuss with you and Christian." I tried to keep my voice level and my thoughts blank. I still wasn't going to let Evie poke around in my head, even if I was planning on telling her everything.

As Evie started to lead us to her office, Christian and Dax appeared from under the stage. The look on his face was one I'd never seen before. I couldn't tell if he was happy or angry at seeing me, but from the rapid drifting of his hair from blonde to brown and back again, I could tell that he wasn't exactly in control of his emotions.

I stared at him with my mouth gaping open, as I had only

learned about drifting during my car ride with Justin. It was obvious why Terrance hadn't wanted to touch on that subject since it would have been apparent that he was one of the bad ones.

"Rose, what on earth are you doing here with him?" Christian didn't sound mad, but he continued to drift as he made his way over to me.

"I have something that I need to talk to you and Evangeline about. Can we please go into her office?" If I waited much longer to get this off my chest, I didn't think I was going to be able to do it.

Evangeline had already moved to hold the door to her office open. Christian grabbed my hand and brought it to his lips. It felt so good to be near him. It was a devastating blow to realize that my plans to become his eternal love had been completely crushed within the last two hours.

"Rose, I'm going to wait in the car with Jillian if that's okay."

Justin gave me a tight smile as he eased his way back outside.

The way Christian was looking at me was starting to freak me out. "Christian, don't worry. There is nothing going on between me and Justin. Just come on...I'll explain everything."

He closed the door as we entered Evangeline's office. Instead of her usual, casual demeanor, Evangeline had her hip propped on the corner of her desk and a bleak look on her face. "Rose, I'd be happy to hear what this is about, so please, without further delay, would you be so kind as to put Christian and my anxiety to rest?"

"I don't really know how to start, so I guess I'll just state the obvious. I know that you are all vampires." I paused and hoped that Justin was right in his assumption that Evangeline wouldn't kill me for knowing their secret.

Christian and Evangeline stared at each other for a few seconds before Christian collapsed into the chair next to me. It took him another moment to turn his head and glare at me.

"How? How do you know? And how long have you been lying to me?"

That was definitely a surprise, and not how I'd expected this conversation to go. His words hit me in the chest like a blow from a prizefighter. "I didn't lie to you. I just didn't tell you that I knew what you were." I had hoped that my confession would be a relief to him, but obviously it was not. "How and when I found out is the reason that I'm here."

Christian looked at me like I was a complete stranger. I had hoped that by me sharing Terrance's deception he would see this as a good thing in the end.

"I found out that vampires existed about seven and a half months ago. I was coming to meet my mom after one of her swim lessons and found a vampire feeding from her instead." I was so nervous to reveal who that vampire was, that in that instant I didn't know if I could do it.

But just then Evangeline moved off her desk and came to

kneel in front of me. "Rose, just tell us everything that happened. I'm not angry with you and you are in no danger from anyone in my clan."

Even though it was Christian that I needed reassurance from, I was thankful to have received it from Evangeline as well. "Thank you. I never meant to deceive anyone. I was just trying to surprise Christian by becoming a vampire, so we could be together forever."

I was hoping that little revelation would soften Christian's opinion of the situation, and from the look he gave me it had worked, if only slightly. The emotions warring across his face were caught somewhere between love and complete disbelief. "How were you going do that Rose? Evie is the only one who can create new vampires."

"I know that now thanks to Justin, but before I was told something different...by Terrance."

At that point Evangeline actually fell backwards, flat onto

her ass. "I knew it!"

I continued in a rush, "I'm sorry I kept it from you, but he told me that if anyone found out that we knew each other or that I knew that vampires existed, that he and I would both be killed. I know now that wasn't true. As a matter of fact, I think everything he told me was a lie. But I just don't understand why he would lie to me. I'm so sorry that I didn't come to you sooner."

Evangeline picked herself up off the floor and leaned against her desk again. "Why don't you tell us exactly how you two met and everything that he told you about us?"

By the time I was done relaying all the lies and promises that Terrance had fed me, Christian and Evangeline both looked completely devastated. Evie had found it especially interesting that Terrance's price for this information was that he be able to continue feeding from my mom.

"I'm sorry if you feel I've lied to you, but I swear I had no idea that what he was telling me was a complete crock of shit. I only found out the truth of how things really worked tonight, and I have Justin to thank for that." I took a deep breath because I had never felt so exhausted in my life.

Evangeline smiled. "Rose, I don't blame you. Terrance was manipulating you, and I have a pretty good idea as to why."

CHAPTER THIRTY

Next Step

(Jeremy/Dad)

"I've called Jillian's house and her parents said that they haven't seen either of them." I didn't know what I was going to do if I didn't find Rose soon. I was so panicked about where she could be and all the bad things that could be happening to her that I had almost called the cops. But thankfully Meredith was there and was trying her best to keep me calm. She had made us some Chamomile tea in an effort to settle my nerves and continued to remind me that Rose was a big girl. Something that I had refused to see for several months now.

"I just can't believe that she ran off. I never imagined that she would actually leave and not come home." It was only about 9 p.m., but it was dark outside and with her last words ringing in my ears, *"Maybe I'll see you at home,"* I was regretting everything that had happened

"Jeremy, I'm sure she's fine. It's obvious that Jillian picked her up and since her parents said she hasn't broken her curfew yet, I'm sure the girls will return soon. I know you're regretting what happened today, but I really do think that everything will be okay."

"Thanks Meredith. I know in my head that you're probably right, but it's convincing my heart that's the problem." I had started to calm down a bit and decided that I would try Rose's cell phone again, when suddenly my phone started ringing in my hand.

"Hello? Rose?"

"No, Jeremy, it's Adrienne Case. I spoke to Jillian and wanted to let you know that the girls are fine. They just finished having dinner with some friends and they asked if Rose could spend the night. I told them that would be fine, but I wanted to let you know in case you wanted to go pick her up instead."

I sat there, relief flowing through my veins like warm whisky. I tried to think what my next step should be. I was so grateful that Rose was okay, but my first instinct was to rush over there and pick her up immediately so that I could see her with my own eyes and continue to explain about Meredith. Then I realized that I should just be grateful Jillian had checked in with her parents. Rose was obviously needing some more time to process everything.

I turned to find Meredith beaming at me. There was no *I told you so* look on her face—just genuine relief and caring. "Thank you, Adrienne. I think it will help Rose to cool down if she can spend the night there, so I appreciate the hospitality. Please let her know that I will be by in the morning to pick her up."

"Sounds good, Jeremy. I'll let her know, and don't worry,

I'm sure this will blow over soon. You two never fight and are as close as can be," she replied. Her response was exactly what I needed to hear.

Once I hung up the phone and reveled in the fact that my only daughter was safe, I turned to face Meredith once more. Suddenly I was overwhelmed with desire, and with Rose not coming home tonight it looked like I was going to break my own rule after all. "Thank you for staying with me through all of this. I never realized how much having you around truly grounded me." I walked to her, preparing to show her just how grateful I was. "Would you do me the pleasure of spending the night with me? Here in my home?"

"I thought you would never ask."

* * * * *

CHAPTER THIRTY-ONE

Demon Downlow

(Rose)

I'm not sure exactly how many times I almost passed out
while listening to Evangeline. She explained what had happened
to Terrance, and the first instinct I had was to run away.

Infected by demon blood? How the hell was I supposed to
process that? I thought I had handled the fact that vampires
existed pretty well, but demons...come on.

And from what Evangeline was saying it was obvious they
thought my mom was the zôt that had infected Terrance. I
actually think I threw up in my mouth a little bit at that
revelation.

"You have to be wrong! You have to be! There is no way that my mother was a fucking demon!"

"Rose, please just calm down. We'll figure this out." Christian was kneeling in front of me, rubbing his hands over my thighs.

I loved that he wanted to help, but I was nowhere close to being consolable. After lifting his hands from my legs, I pushed out of the chair and started to pace. "How am I supposed to calm down? You just told me that you think my mom was a demon, but I'm telling you, there's just no way it's true. She was just my mom. A normal, everyday, suburban mom who taught swim lessons for a living and took care of me and my dad." My dad, oh my God, I wondered if he had any idea.

"Rose, we had initially thought that the woman who infected Terrance had done so maliciously, but from what you're telling us, it seems like it was a simple side-effect from him accidentally encountering her demon blood." I was glad that

Evangeline was no longer blaming my mother for what had happened. "I know this will be hard to deal with, and I'm sorry for having to put you through this, but it's obvious that Terrance is the one who killed your mother."

I sank down to the floor and let Christian wrap me in his arms. I had seen this coming from a mile away, but it still devastated me. I just couldn't understand why he'd done it. Terrance had always treated my mom like something he cherished, so why did he end up killing her instead? Something just didn't seem to be adding up.

Once I regained my balance, I explained that even though he did seem to be the obvious choice, I just couldn't believe that Terrance had been the one to kill my mom.

"Honey, you have to face the facts. Terrance was addicted to the taste of your mother's blood. You said yourself that he told you it was unlike anything he had ever tasted before. He could have easily followed her home after feeding from her one night and found out where you lived and then returned

whenever he wanted. I'm sure that as the poison spread, the

need for her blood became more and more prominent. He

probably just broke into your house to feed from your mom and

finally lost control. Rose, I'm sorry, but you have to agree that

it's the obvious answer and makes perfect sense." Christian had

sped through his explanation. But he was right. Everything that

he was telling me had wrapped my mom's death up in a nice

little bow. Mystery solved.

After a few moments of silence, I resigned myself to face

the facts. "I guess you're right. But what I don't understand is

why he didn't come back for me."

CHAPTER THIRTY-TWO

Regrets

(Jeremy/Dad)

Meredith's and my night had been a whirlwind of passion, but when I woke up to find her sprawled in my bed with her blonde hair spilling over my dead wife's pillow, it had sent a jolt straight through my heart. We had slept together before and spent the night with each other multiple times, but it had always been at her apartment in Masen. So waking up here in the bed that I had shared with my wife for years was something that I clearly hadn't prepared myself for. I suddenly started to have *major* regrets and a *major* change of heart.

"Meredith, I have to go pick up Rose. I'm sorry, but I'm

going to have to ask you to leave." I knew it sounded rude, and I realized that I was taking the coward's way out by using Rose as my excuse to get rid of her. But in reality, I just couldn't bring myself to look at the woman that reminded me of Loraine for a moment longer.

I really don't know what I was thinking by getting involved with her in the first place. Rose was right. I had obviously gravitated towards Meredith because of her looks and how she had reminded me of Loraine. I guess I had been using her to fill the gap that my wife's death had left in my soul.

"I don't have to be back in Masen until tomorrow. Are you sure you don't want me to stick around? I could help explain things between us to Rose, if you'd like." I could see that she was truly trying to be helpful, but I suddenly just couldn't stand the thought of her being around my only daughter.

"No. Thank you, but I really need to speak to Rose alone." I was already heading towards the shower as I took in the hurt expression on her face.

"Jeremy, is everything okay? Have I done something wrong?" Her voice was filled with trepidation.

"Of course not. I'm just anxious to pick up Rose and clear the air between us. I'm sorry if it offends you, but this is something that I need to do alone." I was starting to get angry that I had to justify the fact that this was between me and my daughter. Yes, I knew it concerned her since she was part of the reason Rose had run off in the first place, but since I currently thought that our arrangement was quickly coming to an end, I just couldn't muster up the energy needed to make her feel better.

"Look, Meredith. I'm grateful for the time we've spent together, but after seeing Rose's reaction at the café, it's clear to me that I have rushed into this. I think it would be best if we stopped seeing each other until I can get things settled between Rose and me and truly figure out how I'm feeling." I turned to continue my escape into the bathroom, and that's when I heard the crash.

Seeing the broken vase on the floor alerted me to just how angry she was. "You have got to be fucking kidding me! After everything that I have gone through to be with you, you're going to let your daughter dictate how our relationship is going to go?" She was kneeling on the bed completely naked, which should have been enough of a distraction, but what really had my attention locked in place was the glowing red color that was emanating from her eyes.

CHAPTER THIRTY-THREE

Nowhere To Go

(Rose)

"I'm not sure why Terrance didn't come back to kill you, Rose. It's a completely logical question, but I'm not sure that we will be able to get you an answer to it." Evangeline explained that because of the poison, Terrance was unable to focus on any of the time he'd spent with my mom, the demon. And now that he'd drifted permanently dark and seemed to only have malicious tendencies, Evangeline didn't think that he would be in a sharing mood, even if he could access the memories.

"Couldn't we at least try? Maybe if he sees me and realizes that his deception is no longer a secret, he would open up about it." I couldn't imagine leaving here without some answers.

After hesitating briefly, Christian stood up and took my hand. "I'll take Rose down to question Terrance if you want to stay here and explain to everyone what's happening."

"I'm not sure that's a good idea. You saw how he launched himself at me last night, and I know that he would have attacked Tori earlier if she had gotten any closer." Evangeline was clearly concerned that Terrance was a threat to both Christian and me.

"We won't get close to the cell. Besides, he's still in chains and has nowhere to go. I think it's important that I be the one to escort Rose to see him." Christian's eyes narrowed while he took in Evangeline's concerned expression. It was clear that the two were having some sort of private communication.

"Alright. Come straight back up through my office once you're done. And for God's sake, whatever happens, please make sure you stay out of his reach." Evangeline hugged me and then quickly exited her office, leaving Christian and me standing alone, still holding hands.

"I can't tell you how sorry I am that this is happening to Terrance, and apparently it's all my mom's fault." It was still a hard pill to swallow, but obviously one that I was going to have to get used to.

"Oh, Rose, none of this is your mother's fault. Not really. It seems to me that Terrance just happened to cross paths with her at the pool. Honestly, it could have easily been any one of us." He lifted my face by gently placing his finger under my chin. "I don't blame your mother or you for anything that has happened. And to be really honest, I'm just so happy to hear that you want to become a vampire like me. The thought of spending eternity with you, makes me happier than you can imagine." He bent down and kissed me softly.

I didn't have the words to express how relieved I felt. When this whole fiasco had started, I wasn't sure he was going to forgive me for keeping the truth from him. But now we were both excited to move forward with our lives. I threw my arms around his neck and increased the intensity of our kiss.

"Come on. We have to get down to Terrance and get this over with before the club starts to get busy." He led me over to the book case behind Evangeline's desk and proceeded to push a button under one of the shelves. The bookcase separated, revealing a staircase that led down into a white tiled hallway.

Once we made our way into the rising pit, he led me in the direction of Terrance's cell. I was nervous to see him again, especially now knowing everything I did.

"Are you sure you're going to be up for this? You've experienced quite a few shocks tonight already." Christian stopped and rubbed his hands up and down my arms.

"Yes, I'll be fine. I have to do this." I was tougher than people gave me credit for, and I was about to prove it.

As we rounded the end of the hall and finally came to rest in front of Terrance's cell, we found him sitting on the floor, his back against the wall. His hands and feet were still cuffed in chains. Once he looked up and caught sight of me, he immediately jumped to his feet.

"Obviously you recognize Rose, and the fact that she's here in our pit should be a pretty good indication that your secret is out of the bag." Christian's voice held a sharp tone that had obviously set Terrance on edge. With wide eyes, he frantically kept looking back and forth between the two of us.

"Terrance, why did you lie to me?" I guess if Christian was going to play the bad cop, I was supposed to play the good cop. Not that I wanted to, mind you. I would much rather be playing the bad cop right now. Because honestly, seeing his gorgeous face again and now knowing that he'd been playing me this whole time pissed me off more than I could explain. It actually felt like I was fighting a rising tide of lava that was preparing to explode from within me.

"I'm sorry, Rose. I think she somehow *made* me do it."

Terrance sounded so...normal. I had expected him to be foaming at the mouth and maybe yelling and screaming. But instead, he sounded like his old self: the nice vampire that had opened up my little sheltered world to one of imaginary creatures and the possibility of eternal life.

"What are you saying? She made you lie to me, or she made you kill her?" I wasn't letting him off the hook that easily.

As I waited for his response, I noticed Christian tilting his head with a curious look spreading across his face. I refused to discuss anything in front of Terrance, so I left it for later. "So tell me. Exactly what did my mother make you do?"

"Your mother? What are you talking about?" I guess it was true. The demon blood truly did have a masking effect on Terrance's thoughts and memories.

Unable to control my rage a second longer, I went to take a step towards him when Christian grabbed my arm and shook his head.

"You know exactly what I'm talking about you son of a bitch. You fed from my mother and her demon blood infected you. Then you lied to me about everything. Everything you told me about vampires was a complete load of shit. You never had any intention of changing me, since obviously–YOU CAN'T!" I was shaking with anger by the time I was done and I sunk back into Christian's embrace.

After staring at me for a few seconds, Terrance shook his head. He slid back down to the floor. "I did feed from your mother, and yes, I lied to you. I lied to everyone. But you're wrong...your mom wasn't a demon and I didn't kill her...I loved her."

CHAPTER THIRTY-FOUR

Revelation

(Rose)

After Terrance's revelation, Christian pulled me away from the cell. It was probably because I was dangerously close to losing my temper.

"Why are we leaving? We were just starting to get somewhere." I was desperate to know what Terrance had to say about the events surrounding my mom, especially the part where he'd said she wasn't the demon and that he'd loved her. What the hell?

"I need to talk to Evie before we continue. There is something else going on here, and even though it's still unclear to me, I think it's important to let her know what Terrance has said."

We entered Evangeline's office through the bookcase and then waited for it to close before heading out into the club. It was pretty clear that Christian thought what Terrance had said was somehow important, but I didn't understand why.

After pulling me through the crowd by our clasped hands, Christian approached Dax. "Where's Evie?" Dax almost flinched at the stoic tone in Christian's voice.

"What's wrong?"

"I'm not sure, but I just need to find Evie to discuss something, so where is she?" Christian eased up on the tension a little.

"She's feeding upstairs." Dax looked at me as he said it, probably to gauge my reaction.

Christian only nodded in Dax's direction then proceeded to pull me up the stairs. "Do you want to wait outside?"

I raised my eyebrows at him. Obviously it was going to take everyone a little time to adjust to the fact that they didn't have to hide things from me anymore."I've watched Terrance feed from my mom tons of times, so if it's okay with Evie, I'd like to come."

I loved the look that filled Christian's eyes as he leaned down to kiss me. "There is no way for me to put into words how happy it makes me to finally be able to share every aspect of my life with you."

"I feel the exact same way." I kissed him back, trying to show him exactly how happy our newfound honesty had made me. "I can't wait until all this is over and we can actually start seeing each other on a regular basis again." I knew that right now wasn't the time to discuss it, but the idea of Christian spending the night and day with me in my new apartment was like a little slice of heaven.

"We'd better get in there to tell Evie what happened or else

I'm going to drag you into one of these private rooms and finish what we started the last time I was here." I slid my hands down his chest and I bit my lower lip in an effort to stop myself from kissing him again.

"You're right. But very soon, I *will* be getting you alone." His voice had that sexy, gravely quality that never failed to make me melt.

Christian stepped toward the curtained entrance and lightly called out, "Evie, may we enter? I have some news."

Silence reigned for only a split second. "Yes Christian. Please come in."

I have to admit, when we entered the room I had been a little nervous as to what I was going to see. Watching as Terrance fed from my mom was one thing. It had definitely taken some time to get used to, but after seeing how it really didn't hurt her in any way it had gotten easier. So I was pleasantly surprised to find Evie sitting on the velvet couch with her visitor's wrist pressed to her mouth. She had a little handkerchief that she used to dab the corners of her mouth as she pulled his arm away. She made it look so civilized, so pleasant, and for the first time since learning of their existence, I actually wondered what it would be like to be fed from.

"What news do you have for me?" Evie asked. Her visitor stood up and silently exited the room, leaving the three of us alone.

"Terrance recognized Rose and didn't try to deny it when he saw her. But the really interesting part is that when Rose questioned him about her mom, he was able to focus on the memories and actually told us that she wasn't the demon and that he didn't kill her, but that he had actually been in love with her."

The confused look on Evie's face resembled the jumbled mess of thoughts that was currently rattling around in my head. I didn't see how this meant anything other than Terrance was still obviously lying to everyone.

"That is extremely interesting and disconcerting at the same time." Evie stood and started pacing the luxurious room.

"No offense, but what the fuck does that mean?" I was getting tired of feeling like I was being left in the dark.

"Whenever I question Terrance about the woman I see in his thoughts, the one he was feeding from, the images are always blocked or fuzzy. When you told us that Terrance had been feeding from your mom it just seemed clear that your mom was the demon. But now I'm not so sure. Because if she had been the demon, he wouldn't have been able to focus or talk about her in any way."

"What? I don't understand. You said that my mom was the demon and that feeding from her is what caused Terrance to drift dark and do the things he's been doing. Now you're saying that it wasn't my mom?" I would be absolutely thrilled if it turned out my mom wasn't to blame, but it still didn't clear up all the questions as to who was responsible and how it was connected to my mom's death.

"What exactly did Terrance say?" Evie leaned back on the couch and crossed her legs.

"He said, 'I did feed from your mother, and yes, I lied to you. I lied to everyone. But you're wrong...your mom wasn't a demon and I didn't kill her...I loved her.'" Christian's verbatim account of what Terrance had told us seemed to leave Evie with even more to think about.

"There's something else." Christian's statement had me on high alert. I couldn't imagine what he was going to say, since Terrance hadn't said anything else to us.

"What is it?" Evie asked. She was apparently just as curious as I was.

"I think my new ability, the one you said I'm developing, somehow worked while we were with Terrance. I can't explain it, but for some reason, I just *know* that Rose's mother wasn't the demon. Terrance was telling the truth."

CHAPTER THIRTY-FIVE

True Love

(Jeremy/Dad)

The moment I spun around to face Meredith's rage I swore that her eyes had been glowing red. But once I refocused, it was clear that it had only been a play of light from the red vase that she'd smashed on the floor. The sun was streaming in through the bedroom windows and had apparently hit the vase just right, lighting up her face in scary relief.

"Answer me! Are you seriously going to let your daughter control how you live your life?" She was clearly still upset but had sunken back down onto the bed and covered herself up with the sheets.

"I'm sorry if this is hard for you. But you have to understand, Rose *is* my life. She's my only family now, and I will always put her first." I tried to speak calmly in order to soften the blow, but I wasn't in the mood to coddle her. We were both adults and it wasn't like this was true love. I had already had that once in my life and I knew nothing else would ever come close again. "I'm going to get in the shower, and then I'm going to go pick up my daughter. You're more than welcome to wait until I leave and I'll walk you out, or you can just go and I'll call you later this week. It's up to you."

I heard her quiet sobs as I shut the bathroom door. I knew I should feel worse than I did, but the only thing I could concentrate on right now, was getting to my daughter and apologizing for being such a terrible father.

* * * * *

(Meredith)

The moment Jeremy shut the bathroom door I tried to dry my tears. I couldn't believe this was happening. After everything I had gone through to be with him, one little hissy fit from his daughter ruins everything. I just couldn't allow that.

I got dressed and gathered my things. There was no way I was going to wait around so he could walk me out, carting me to the curb like a piece of fucking trash. Screw this! I'd leave alright, but you could damn sure bet I'd be back.

* * * * *

(Jeremy/Dad)

Meredith was gone by the time I finished my shower and got dressed. I couldn't pretend that I wasn't relieved. I really did need to get to Rose and make sure that she was okay. I noticed that I had missed a call from her, so I was hopeful that we would be able to work things out today. But for some reason, my anxiety had ratcheted up a few notches since last night. I hadn't gotten any other reports from Adrienne, so I assumed the girls were fine, but I just couldn't settle my thoughts. The urgent feeling to reach Rose was quickly climbing to an uncontrollable level.

As I rounded the corner, I saw Jillian's car in the Case's driveway. This was a good sign and definitely helped to relieve my stress. I parked and headed towards the front door. Just as I was reaching for the bell, the door opened and out walked Jillian.

"Good morning, Mr. Reynolds." She was dressed in her usual sporty attire and seemed bright-eyed and bushy-tailed. I had expected to see Rose following closely behind, but instead Jillian shut the door and started towards her car.

"Morning, Jillian. Where's Rose?" So much for my stress levels staying in check.

"She actually took the bus to school this morning. She said to let you know that she's not quite ready to talk and that car shopping will have to wait. She said that she'll see you at home tonight though." Her words hit me hard.

I guess I should have expected it, but the news of her heading to school to avoid me really hurt. I had been looking forward to telling her how sorry I was, and that I had called it off with Meredith, but obviously that would have to wait until tonight. "Well, thank you for the message Jillian I won't keep you."

I headed back to my car, wondering just what I should do to fill my day. I rarely took days off from work. I was never sick, and since Loraine died, unless Rose was home, I didn't really enjoy being in the house alone. So with the entire day to myself, I decided to head to the gym to clear my head. After pumping some iron I should be a little less stressed and then maybe I would go looking for Rose's new car anyway. Anything to pass the time.

CHAPTER THIRTY-SIX

Deal with the Bad Stuff

(Rose)

Christian, Evangeline, and I were still sitting in the private room of The Rising Pit when Dax entered the room. "What's happened?"

Evie smiled at her consort and began to explain. "When Christian and Rose went to question Terrance, he didn't deny that he recognized her. He was also able to focus on Rose's mother and he admitted that he had in fact fed from her." Dax sank into the chaise opposite Christian as Evie continued. "Terrance told them that Rose's mom wasn't the demon."

"Do you believe him?" Dax asked.

"Thanks to Christian's new developing ability, yes, I do."

I hadn't had the chance to ask Christian what they were talking about yet. It sounded like a good thing and something that Evie was coming to rely on, so I decided to let it go. We definitely needed to deal with the bad stuff before we could get to the good.

"So if Rose's mother wasn't the demon, then who was? And why were they having Terrance manipulate and lie to Rose?" Dax asked.

"I'm not sure. It could be that the two things aren't even related. Terrance could have fed from this demon, and then once he started to permanently drift, the lying and manipulation just came as a natural part of him going dark." Evie stood and made her way to take a seat at the end of Dax's chaise. "This could actually be good news for everyone. Not only is Rose's mother not the demon, but now we have a chance of finding this woman alive. And, maybe that means we can still find a way to save him." She leaned down and kissed Dax's cheek.

We sat there in silence for a few moments, which allowed me to try to put all the pieces together in my head. Finally, I came to the one question that I just hadn't figured out. "I know you said that you thought my mom was the demon because of the timing of everything: Terrance's feeding from her, her death, and his drifting. But if you've seen this woman in his thoughts, then shouldn't you have known that it wasn't my mom from the beginning?"

"Well no, Rose. Actually it was quite the opposite. When you were explaining everything that had happened and when you described your mother's appearance, it made perfect sense. The woman I saw in Terrance's thoughts were just as you described: tall, thin, and with long, blonde hair."

It took me a moment to process what Evie had said. Tall, thin, and with long, blonde hair. *Holy shit!* "I can't believe this. I know who the demon is!" I jumped up and reached for my cell phone. I had to call my dad and warn him that the bitch he was seeing was actually a demon. "I just met my dad's new girlfriend, and you wouldn't believe how much she looks just like my mom." I was going to nail that bitch to the wall.

"Rose, come here." Christian grabbed my hand and guided me back down on the couch next to him. "Think about this for a minute. The only reason that we thought it was your mother was because of all the other coincidences. This woman you are referring to could just be another person with blonde hair. It's most likely that she has nothing to do with it."

I knew that he was making sense. I mean, it wasn't like my mom and Meredith were the only two women in the world with long blonde hair and tall thin bodies. But for some reason I really thought I was on to something. "I don't know Christian. It just seems too much of a coincidence that she came into my dad's life right after my mom was killed and all this was happening around the same time as when Terrance drifted dark.

I really do think there's a connection."

"We can't afford not to check it out," Evie said. "Rose, it's almost sunrise, so why don't you borrow Christian's car and head to school? See if you can use the library at the college to dig up anything on this Meredith woman. I had Justin take Jillian home and use his sedative to convince her and her parents to give your dad a cover story. And if I were you, I would probably avoid seeing your dad until we get this figured out. I'll leave a key to the club for you with Dominique. Pick it up on your way out. That way you can come straight back here afterwards."

Evie stood and walked towards me. "I can't tell you how happy I am that you and Christian finally have things out in the open. Normally, he would have been required to keep our secret from you until the new Sire is chosen, but since you came to us, there are no rules that have been broken. I'm very happy for the two of you." She kissed my cheek and then headed for the door with Dax following closely behind.

I never expected for Evie to be so gracious in welcoming me. As a matter of fact, I had thought she was going to rip my head off the second she heard I knew vampires existed. I sat back down next to Christian on the couch.

Christian's hair and eyes started to drift as soon as I sat down. I wasn't one hundred percent sure how this drifting thing worked yet, so I wasn't sure if this was a good sign or a bad one. "What is it?"

"It just makes me so angry that all of Terrance's lies have left you with such a violent and completely distorted vision of us." He ran his hand down the side of my arm.

"I know it will take some time for me to sort through all the lies, but I'm really glad that I finally told you the truth, but this also means that I won't be surprising you by becoming a vampire any time soon." I reached up and touched his cheek. I couldn't wait to start my forever life with him and it almost brought me to tears to think that there was no way to make that happen sooner.

"I wouldn't be so sure about that." Christian's response had me confused but filled with hope at the same time.

"What do you mean?"

"Do you remember when Evie and I were talking about my 'new developing ability'? Well, Evie thinks I'm showing signs of being triggered. Which if it's true, means that I'm in line to become the next Sire."

I about fell off the couch at Christian's revelation. Holy shit. My boyfriend was going to be the next Sire, and that meant...he could be the one to change me. The coming morning had just started to look a whole lot brighter.

CHAPTER THIRTY-SEVEN

Digging for Dirt

(Rose)

I was so tired after being up for twenty-four hours, but there was no way that I could sleep with the idea that my dad's new girlfriend was the demon that had infected Terrance. So, instead of heading home to catch a few hours of sleep, I headed straight for school like Evie had suggested.

Once I'd gotten there, I was happy to see that Mr. Thompson had assigned open study time for his class today. He was notorious for doing that when it was so close to graduation in order to give any of the slackers time to ask questions and really buckle down on their papers. Luckily I was not one of the slackers and was way ahead of the game when it came to my thesis, but Mr. Thompson didn't need to know that.

"Mr. Thompson, may I have a pass to the library for the rest of the day? I've really fallen behind and there are quite a few points that I need to double check." Thank goodness the only problem I had ever caused in his class was one that I had recently created myself.

"Of course. I wouldn't want one of my best students to not have her thesis completed on time." Mr. Thompson wrote me the pass, so I was set to hang in the library for the rest of the day. Now I just hoped that it wasn't going to be a huge waste of time. I really did think that Meredith was the one we were looking for and if I had to spend an entire day digging for dirt on her, then that's exactly what I would do.

* * * * *

(Meredith)

The moment I crossed the bridge back into Masen, I headed straight for my apartment. I couldn't believe that Jeremy had kicked me out and called things off between us.

There was no way that I was letting that half-breed daughter of his ruin everything that I had gone through to get to him.

I remembered the day that Jeremy Reynolds had walked into my office over a year ago. Tall, confident, and gorgeous as hell. I had sensed right off that he was a demon, but after spending a few hours in his presence, it was clear that he had no idea.

I knew there were other demon bloodlines out there besides my family, but Jeremy was the first one that I had ever run across, which had meant that I'd have a shot at continuing a pure demon bloodline. The only thing I needed to do was get Mr.

Reynolds into my bed.

After a few business meetings that I had manipulated, Jeremy became the head of all of our marketing campaigns. That meant that he would be spending a lot of time here in Masen and a lot more time with me. And time was exactly what I needed if I was going to figure out a plan to get him to cheat on his wife.

Everything had been going great during our business meetings. I had gotten to know him over long phone calls, video conference calls, and of course the monthly, overnight meetings here in Masen. But the one thing that I had learned from all this time spent together was that he loved his wife with all his heart. She was a swim instructor and they enjoyed a simple life, raising their daughter in their family home. How picture perfect. Too bad none of them knew the truth about themselves or the world around them.

It hadn't taken me long to find a vampire clan close to

Jeremy's home. So once I had visited The Rising Pit and chose the vampire that I wanted to do my dirty work, I offered myself to be his visitor for the night. Terrance had been more than willing to escort me to one of the private rooms.

Once he had set his fangs in my neck and began taking long draws of my blood, I could sense right when my demon blood had started to infect him. I had gone back a few times after that, knowing that my blood would have caused his memories of me to be hazy. So we repeated the processes again and again, making sure that he was well on his way to drifting dark.

I had learned of the old stories and demon histories from my mother, as she had learned them from her mother, who had learned them from her mother. But I wasn't completely sure this would work since there hadn't been a record of it in over 100,000 years. It was actually pretty rare that there was anyone left who truly knew that the demon/human bloodline even existed.

There were cases every now and again in the bigger clans where a vampire had accidentally bitten a demon while feeding and had drifted dark, but the cases were few and far between and the vampires had no idea what had caused the odd events. And since they could never figure out why it happened, their "rule" was to deliver the true death to any vampires that had drifted permanently dark. It was so convenient. By killing their infected vampires, the clans were helping to keep our race hidden from the world without even knowing it.

I had thought that I would be able to control Terrance since he'd been infected with my blood. All I would've had to do was give him suggestions through the mind bond we shared and he would do anything I asked. The poison would then conveniently wipe it from his memory.

I had never imagined that Terrance would have fallen in love with Loraine. I guess I should have known something was off when he first reported that her blood tasted different to him.

He'd been more than willing to continue to feed from her and keep her occupied while I'd arranged late night meetings with Jeremy. When Rose discovered him, the easiest thing to do was to have him continue to keep both of them occupied by lying and feeding her fantasies of becoming a vampire. It had given me plenty of time to continue to lure Jeremy into my bed.

At first, I really didn't have any desire to actually kill Loraine, but once I noticed that Terrance was close to completely drifting dark, I knew it was only a matter of time before his Sire delivered the true death. So, unless I got Jeremy to sleep with me before that happened, I was going to be forced to find another vampire to continue this charade. And now that Rose had gotten involved, I knew it would be easier to just get rid of Loraine altogether. Besides, I had really grown fond of Jeremy and could see myself building a life with him instead of just a one night stand. Plus, I wasn't even sure that I would get pregnant during our first encounter, and who knew if I'd ever convince him to sleep with me again. No, getting rid of Loraine was the only thing that I could do.

At the time I had thought that Terrance would of course be the one to do it. It could've easily been a "side-effect" of his drifting dark. He would just happen to lose control while feeding from her, but with his emotions so deeply involved, I wasn't completely sure that my mind bond would be strong enough to actually force him to kill the woman that he loved. Plus, there was the problem of dealing with Rose. My initial thought had been for Terrance to just bite her and use his sedative to make her forget, but then I had remembered she was half-demon. I had no idea if Rose's blood contained enough poison to give her control over Terrance and I wasn't willing to risk it. No, it had turned out that I would have to be the one to take care of things myself.

(Rose)

After digging for the first three hours, I had found nothing incriminating on Meredith Karver. I had at least found out what her last name was. It had been easy enough as I knew she worked for a company in Masen that was one of my dad's clients.

Since my initial discovery however, I hadn't run across anything else of use. I traced her family back to the southern area of New Mexico, but if what Evie had told me held true, the demon families would have scattered across the world throughout history, so knowing where she came from really wasn't going to make much of a difference.

Now that I was completely out of ideas as to what the hell I should be looking for, combined with the fact that I'd been up for over twenty-four hours straight, exhaustion was really starting to set in.

I didn't want to risk seeing my dad yet, so I decided to head back to the club like Evie had suggested and get some sleep. I figured that way I would be there when the clan woke up and I could inform them that my little research trip had been a complete waste of time.

I gathered up my books and headed down the hall just as the bell rang. The halls filled up with commotion, so I didn't really notice when Jillian had slid up next to me.

"Hi!" She certainly sounded like she had gotten enough sleep last night. Lucky bitch.

"Hey, how are you?"

"I'm okay. Last night was fun, huh?" The look she was giving me was freaking me out. I knew that Justin had given them some kind of cover story, but I hadn't exactly gotten all the details.

"Um, yeah...it was great!" I decided that sticking to vague

answers was the way to go.

"We should road trip more often. Then that delicious dinner we had with our friends...YUM! We are so going back to that restaurant. Actually, remember Mom said that we could probably go back this weekend when you spend the night again. Anyway, I can't wait. Catch ya later!" She bounded off in a flurry of ponytail swishes and tennis shoe squeaks. I assumed that Justin had removed himself from the story last night which was fine by me. I really didn't want to have to start explaining things to Jillian too. So right now, I was utterly happy to leave her in her bubble of ignorance.

CHAPTER THIRTY-EIGHT

Follow My Gut

(Rose)

When I arrived back at the club, I used the key that Evie had given me to let myself in. It was so odd being here during the day, knowing that everyone was below sleeping in the pit, including Christian.

It only took me a few seconds to find the button that he had used before to open the bookcase in Evie's office. I figured if I was here and was going to be getting some sleep, I wanted to be doing it in my boyfriend's bed.

Thankfully, finding Christian's room had only taken me opening one wrong door. I had found Bobby sprawled across his bed, fully clothed, thank God. The next door I opened revealed Christian. He was lying on his back in only a pair of snug fitting boxers and no shirt. The sight of him took my breath away.

I wasn't exactly sure how this would go, but since I assumed that he really did mean *dead to the world*, I didn't think I would disturb him as I climbed into bed.

He wasn't cold or stiff...ahem. I maneuvered him out of the way as I made room for myself and curled up next to him.

It felt so perfect to finally be resting in the arms of my boyfriend, that at this point it truly didn't even register that he was a vampire. Christian, and everyone in his clan for that matter, had always been completely nice to me, Terrance notwithstanding. They had never once made fun of me or showered me with pity because of what had happened. In truth, these vampires were nicer than most of the humans that I knew, and I couldn't wait to become part of their clan.

I let these thoughts fill my head as I started to drift off to sleep. What better way to spend my dreaming hours than imagining myself as part of Christian's life forever.

* * * * *

(Christian)

The moment I started to rise from being comatose, I knew something was different. As usual, the image that formed in my head was of Rose, since she was the last thing I had thought of before lying down. But this was different. It was like I could actually smell her.

The moment that I broke through into consciousness, I realized that Rose was actually here in my bed, snuggled up against me, sleeping softly. *My God, what did I do to deserve such a reward?*

This was how I wanted to wake for the rest of my existence: Rose's beautiful blonde hair, pouring over her shoulders and onto my arms. Her sweet scent filling my nose, her sexy body pressed into me just right. Damn, I had never wanted anything more than I wanted her in that moment.

I decided to follow my gut and reached around to smooth her hair away from her face. She started to stir as I kissed my way down her neck. "Good evening, angel."

"Mmmm. Good evening indeed." Her voice was sultry and smooth as honey as she started to wake. The way her body moved and curved as she twisted around to face me sent delicious shocks racing along my nerves. I was ready for her in an instant.

She must have felt my growing need. "Mmmm...this is exactly what I was just dreaming about," she said.

I was so on fire that I couldn't even reply. I continued to kiss and caress my way down Rose's body, making sure to soak up every single inch as we peeled each other out of our remaining clothes.

"Are you sure we have time for this?" Rose asked.

As I looked up and met her heavy-lidded eyes, she must have taken in my darkened appearance, because a sexy smile spread across her mouth. One that made me ache to kiss her until we were both left breathless.

"And here I thought it was a bad thing when you drifted dark." She giggled between kisses, while continuing to run her hands down my back.

With the level of emotion that I was feeling right now, I was probably as dark as Terrance. But this kind of drifting had nothing to do with demons, or poison, but instead an intense desire and passion that stemmed from the love I felt for Rose.

"I love you Rose. I love you with everything that I am, which may not be much, but it's all yours." I knew that sounded stupid and sappy the moment it left my lips, but it was the truth.

In that instant I knew that I'd give her everything and anything she ever wanted. I refused to live without her.

"I love you too, Christian. And I'm yours, now, and soon to be forever. Will you please make love to me?"

CHAPTER THIRTY-NINE

New Life

(Jeremy/Dad)

After spending the rest of the afternoon car shopping for Rose, I decided that it just wouldn't be right for me to pick out her first car for her or to use it to try to smooth things over between us. I've never had to buy my daughters affection in the past, and I certainly wasn't going to start now.

So after a quick shower, I made myself a sandwich and waited for Rose to come home from school.

I thought things would go pretty smoothly after I had the chance to tell her that I had broken things off with Meredith, but I wasn't stupid. I knew she felt betrayed that I had kept my relationship a secret in the first place. And the even bigger hurdle was that I was sure she was feeling very protective of her mother's memory. Who could blame her?

I had never truly expected to start dating Meredith after Loraine's death but while dealing with my grief she listened, consoled, made me laugh, and encouraged me to focus on Rose. I was truly grateful to her for helping me deal with the pain.

Then one night, during my overnight meeting in Masen, she had expressed her feelings for me. I remember being a little surprised, but not really. She always seemed to have that glint in her eye; the one that makes it pretty clear to any man when a woman is interested in him. She had told me that listening to me talk about Loraine and Rose had made her realize what a wonderful man I was, and that she couldn't deny that she was developing feelings for me. She also said that if I felt she was being disrespectful of Loraine's memory that she would understand if I wanted to end things.

But I should have been stronger. The truth was, as much as I liked Meredith as a person, it was because she reminded me of Loraine that I fell into her bed.

Thinking back now, it had been wonderful and just what I needed at that time. I know that made me sound like a terrible person, but the truth was, if I hadn't had Meredith to turn to during these past months, I probably would have just withered away, or even worse, been more obsessive about Rose's life than I already had been.

I knew Rose humored me by letting my driver take her and pick her up from school. And she was always such a sweet girl about following my insane rules when it came to her safety. If I was being honest with myself, I knew it was only a matter of time before she snapped. I'm actually pretty surprised it took this long.

But now we could clear the slate and have a fresh start. I realized that my overprotectiveness was only going to push her away, so it was time I let my little girl grow up. I needed to start

a new life, too. I couldn't continue to fake my way through a

relationship with a woman who looked like Loraine. It was time

to move on.

* * * * *

(Meredith)

I had to figure out a way to get Jeremy back. Not only to

continue my pure demon bloodline, but because I had truly

fallen in love with him. I had never met anyone so dedicated to

his family. He was the perfect man: tall, dark, handsome...smart,

sophisticated, and sexy. I absolutely refused to let him go. But

how? How was I supposed to get around the fact that he was

now focused on his daughter and her feelings about our

relationship? What a bunch of bullshit. The girl was almost

twenty-one and would very soon be staying twenty-one forever.
I had to get back into Jeremy's life, because when Rose turned
into a vampire, he was going to be devastated all over again, and
just like last time...I'd be there to pick up the pieces.

But who knew how long it would take for Rose to actually
get accepted into the clan and changed, or what effect the
change would have on her? Word on the street was that
Evangeline couldn't sire any more new vamps and their new Sire
hadn't been triggered yet. I supposed I could get rid of her the
same way I did her mom. It hadn't really been all that hard when
the time had come to finally do it.

Since I knew where Terrance met Rose and Loraine, I had
waited in the parking lot of the swim complex until he'd finished
feeding and then I had used my mind bond with him to instruct
Loraine to leave her bedroom at 2 a.m. Once everyone had gone
their separate ways, I followed Loraine and Rose back to their
house.

I only had to wait a few hours, and then right before 2 a.m., I broke in. She was coming out of her room just as instructed. I figured that I would use the recently closed puncture wounds that Terrance had left to make it look like a vampire draining. Demons don't have fangs like vampires, but our incisors are sharp enough that if we want to drink blood like our ancestors had, we definitely had the ability. I remember when my grandmother had first told me that drinking human blood was not only the way of our demon ancestors, but that they'd believed it filled them with the essence of the person from whom they drank. I figured in this case, since I already looked enough like Loraine, it could only help me to actually ingest her essence while I eliminated her.

Once she had been drained, I remembered leaving with the feeling that I had just come home. Whether it was her essence already flowing through me or the fact that I now knew that Jeremy and I would be building a life together, it had been euphoric. Getting rid of Loraine had been the best idea I had ever had.

But getting rid of Rose was a different story. I couldn't risk biting her in order to kill her like I had her mom. Since she was a half-demon, there was a possibility that her blood would actually allow her control over me if I were to ingest it. I wasn't going to be able to control her in any way since she wasn't a vampire yet, so I had no way to infect her with my poison like I had with Terrance. I had no idea how this was going to work.

I knew she wouldn't willingly help me get back on Jeremy's good side, so I was going to have to come up with a different plan all together: one that would put me back in Jeremy's life and eliminate Rose's hold over him.

I'd already decided that infecting another vampire was too much trouble at this point, so the only option I had left was to threaten Rose and turn her father against her. I had thought about simply killing her in a more modern way, like shooting her, or a random stabbing at her college, but as much as I wanted her gone so I could build a life with Jeremy, I didn't want to risk starting a war with the vampires. I knew that Rose's death would put them on the hunt, and with Terrance still alive, it would only be a matter of time before they found me out.

CHAPTER FORTY

Fire in My Veins

(Rose)

After reveling in the best experience of my life, Christian and I laid in his bed, kissing and snuggling like two newlyweds.

"I wish we could stay like this all night and do that over and over." I nipped little kisses along his jaw line. God, I just couldn't keep my hands or lips off of him. "God, you are the most delicious thing I have ever tasted."

He laughed. "That's something the vampire should be saying to you, not the other way around."

The smile on his face kept the comment light, but the reality of it hit me right away. "Do you want to feed from me?"

He started drifting the moment the words left my mouth. His hair got darker and his eyes started to lose their caramel swirl, and since everything I had learned about vampires had been completely wrong, I didn't know if I should start to panic or not. But then my heart caught up with my head and I realized that Christian would never do anything to hurt me.

"I assume since you're drifting that it means you're hungry?" I wasn't sure if I was making a mistake by talking about it so openly, but what the hell...I was tired of keeping secrets, especially if I was going to become a vampire soon, too.

"Yes, I'm hungry. Horny, too! The thought of feeding from you is a most delectable idea and it's playing havoc with my brain as well as other parts of my body." He sat up and scooted closer to me. "Before you knew that I was a vampire, it was forbidden for me to feed from you because I was in love with you. When a vampire feeds from the one he loves, there is no sedative that can make you forget. So if I were to have fed from you, you would have immediately known I was a vampire, and revealing ourselves is something that no clan permits."

"I guess it's a good thing that I figured it out all on my own then, huh?" I smiled as he leaned in to kiss me. "So now that everything is out in the open you can feed from me without getting in trouble?"

"Yes." His voice was low and steady, but I could tell that he was actually straining for control.

I loved having this much power over him. To know that it was me he loved and craved in so many ways was definitely a turn-on. So with a surge of excitement burning like fire in my veins, I let the sheet drop back onto the bed, revealing my breasts as I tilted my head." So go on then...feed."

(Christian)

It was taking every ounce of will power I had to stop myself from launching at Rose. With her beautiful breasts, the memory of what we had just done etched in my brain, and the pumping of blood just below her beautiful neck...this was excruciating!

But the moment I started to consider her offer, my "new ability" must have kicked in. Because not only did I know that this wouldn't be the right time, but that it would in fact be a huge mistake. I didn't know why, and I didn't know how I was going to explain it to Rose, but I knew, completely one hundred percent knew, that I shouldn't feed from my girlfriend.

"Rose, I can't tell you how tempting you are right now, but we really don't have time for me to feed. I can hear Evie and the others starting to gather, and they know you are here. They're very anxious to hear what you found out. I'm sorry." I peeled myself from the bed and dressed in a flash of vampire speed.

Now who was the one hiding things?

As we made our way up into the club, Rose had seemed quiet. I'm sure it was because of my rejection, but there was just nothing else I could do. I also knew that I was going to have to tell Evie what had happened.

When we reached the top of the stairs and exited from under the stage, the smiles that greeted us were a good sign that everyone would be accepting Rose into the clan. "Look what the cat drug in," Tori teased.

Rose smiled and scooted tighter against my body. "Hi, everyone."

Evie moved towards us and reached out to hug Rose. "I can't tell you how it does my heart good to see you wake with Christian. And hopefully soon, we can make that a permanent thing."

Everyone gave their whoops and cat calls in agreement. I

was so proud to have Rose on my arm.

"So, Rose, what did you find out about Meredith?" Evie motioned for all us to take a seat.

"Unfortunately, nothing. I found out her last name and that her family was originally from the southern part of New Mexico, but I don't see how either of those things is going to help us in any way." I could tell Rose felt bad for not having more valuable information to share.

"Well, that's okay. I think that we definitely need to keep an eye on her though, so I'm going to send for Renard and Loni. They are traveling in Europe at the moment, but I know they will be more than willing to cut their honeymoon short once they find out about the situation that we're facing." Evie finished by telling Rose she could use the key to the club she'd given her whenever she wanted, and now that she knew of our existence, she could join us when the club was open as well. Since we no longer had to hide our true selves from her, it would be easy to bite and sedate any law enforcement that would question her presence in the club.

As everyone headed off to start opening the club, I pulled Rose close. "Are you going to be okay to go home and face your dad? He's probably pretty worried about you by now."

"Yes. I should be fine. I'm going to call him on my way and make sure that the demon bitch isn't going to be there, and then maybe once we're alone I can talk some sense into him." She rose up onto her tippy toes and kissed me goodbye. "Thanks for an amazing night. I love you."

"I love you too. Call me if you need anything. I can literally be there in flash." I was so reluctant to let her go, but I knew it was necessary.

* * * * *

CHAPTER FORTY-ONE

Father–Daughter Moment

(Jeremy/Dad)

Once five o'clock ticked by, I realized that Rose wasn't
coming straight home after school. I had tried her phone, but
there was no answer. I called Jillian's house, and as expected,
everyone was out. I hoped that maybe Rose was with them and
not somewhere on her own, but honestly, I knew better. I didn't
think that she was doing anything bad, but just taking more time
to wrap her head around everything that had happened. But
damn it...if she'd only come home or pick up her phone then I
could tell her that there was nothing to be upset about, and that
Meredith and I were over.

I literally sat there stewing, pacing, cussing and almost crying for another two hours before she called.

"I'll be home soon." she said. She was safe and sounded fine, but it was obvious by the tone in her voice that she was nervous. It made my heart tighten.

Throughout our entire lives, Rose and I had been extremely close. She wasn't exactly a daddy's girl, because she had been just as close to her mother, but that was the beauty of it. We had had the perfect family. Then Loraine was murdered, and even though Rose and I remained close, there was a distance that Loraine's death had put between us, and I was coming to realize that it was probably all my fault.

I didn't know how else to behave. Protecting my daughter was an almost primal instinct. But I had to admit, I shouldn't have been so overbearing. I just hope I hadn't realized it too late.

"Okay, honey. I'll be waiting. See you soon." I tried to keep it light and not indicate just how upset I was.

By the time I heard a car pull up in the driveway, I had practically worn a path into the carpet between the living room and the front door. When the car didn't pull off again, I realized that this wasn't Jillian dropping her off, but was in fact Rose herself. That must have been where she went after school...to buy her new car.

I tried not to let it hurt, but it was something that I really had wanted to do with her, and now her anger had robbed us of that father daughter moment. But since there was nothing I could do about it now, I supposed as long as it was a dependable car then I was just going to have to let it go.

When I peeked out the window and saw a suped-up muscle car instead, I almost passed out. This was so unlike Rose. I suddenly wasn't too sure that our conversation was going to go so well after all.

* * * * *

(Rose)

The entire time I was driving towards home, I kept trying to think of a reasonable excuse for my dad not to see Meredith. But honestly, besides the fact that I thought she was a demon, everything else I came up with just made me sound like a spoiled brat who was upset that her daddy had moved on with his life. Which, when I think about it is pretty damn ironic, since that's exactly what I'd been complaining about for months.

The moment I pulled up into our driveway, I stopped thinking about what to say about Meredith, and instead wondered what the hell I was going to say about Christian's car. Then again, I was so over this whole "sweet innocent Rose" persona that everyone had always put upon me, that I was actually looking forward to telling the truth. Coming out to Christian and his clan had been a truly freeing experience. Now,

I just had to see how well I could pull it off with my dad.

As soon as I opened the front door, I saw him sitting on the living room couch. "Hey Dad," I said. I really didn't know how to start, or what the fuck I was supposed to say to convince him to not see that bitch ever again, but I had to start somewhere.

"I'm sorry that I ran off after our fight about Meredith. But Dad, you have to see how upsetting it was to realize that not only were you seeing someone and keeping it from me, but that the woman you were seeing looks almost exactly like Mom. How did you think I would react?" I flopped down into the chair opposite his.

"Rose, I understand why you were upset, but I cannot excuse the way that you reacted. We will talk about my relationship with Meredith. But first, we're going to discuss where you've been and why there's a hot-rod sitting in my driveway." Dad was stern but not mad, so I guess it was time for the truth.

"It's my boyfriend's car. Remember, Christian? He was the boy that I was seeing before you tried to turn me into a nun." I guess the truth was going to come with a bite as well.

"I guess I hadn't realized that you were still seeing him. I'm sorry." Dad really did look sorry, and like he hadn't slept very well.

I could tell there was something on his mind and I really wasn't in the mood to drag this out. "Why don't we just get this over with? I'm tired and I have to study for an exam."

"Okay. Well, first of all I'd like to let you know that I've broken things off with Meredith. I know that doesn't excuse that I kept our relationship hidden in the first place, but I just wanted you to know that before I tried to explain anything."

I couldn't believe that this had happened. How perfect. Now I didn't have to play games in order to convince him to dump that bitch.

As I sat back in the chair feeling better than I had only

moments before, Dad continued. "I met Meredith over a year ago, and while she does have traits similar to your mother's, the two of them are nothing alike. Besides, you know how much I loved your mom. But when your mom passed, I didn't think it was fair to bombard you with the pain I was feeling, so I turned to Meredith since we were already close friends. She was understanding, and really helped me process some of the emotions I was feeling as a man who had lost his spouse. Only after I realized that she had developed feelings for me did things turn intimate." He took a deep breath and scooted to the edge of the couch. "I know that it doesn't excuse what I did, but Rose, I'm an adult, and to be honest, I don't have to justify my actions to you. But I want you to understand that at that time I did not think that I was using Meredith to fill the hole your Mother's death left within me. But now, looking back, I think that is exactly what happened."

Dad sat back on the couch and I watched all the air leave

his lungs in a big rush. That must have been what he wanted to get off his chest. I was just so happy that he had called things off with that demon whore that I really didn't need to hear any more. "Dad, I'm sorry for overreacting. You're right. You're an adult and you don't have to justify anything to me. I guess that I just felt hurt by the fact that you thought you needed to keep it a secret in the first place. But with how much Meredith looked like Mom, I guess I can understand that it was a difficult position for you to be in." I walked over and sat down on the couch next to him and gave him a hug. "I love you. And I do want you to be happy, just not with a woman that looks like Mom. I just don't think it's good for you, or for me."

"I love you too, Rose. And thank you for understanding that even adults can make mistakes, especially when our hearts are involved." Dad kissed the top of my head and then guided us up off the couch. "Let's head to bed. All this worrying and fretting has left me exhausted, and you said you have a test to study for, right?"

"I do. But one last thing. Are we okay with me having my freedom back? I really don't want to fight with you anymore." I tried to say it jokingly, but I was dead serious.

"Yes, honey. I am okay with you having your freedom back. I'll let Dennis know tomorrow morning that he will no longer be driving for you. But...I really do think we need to get you a car of your own, because the thought of you zooming around in that thing out there completely terrifies me."

I laughed as I hugged him again. "Okay. Sounds good. Can we plan on car shopping after you get off work tomorrow? I'll meet you back here and then we can head out."

"Sounds good to me."

I didn't know what was going to happen with Meredith or with Christian and me, but it made me feel good that me and my dad were on good terms again. Too bad that it couldn't last.

CHAPTER FORTY-TWO

Better Plan

(Meredith)

It's about fucking time. The moment that I saw Jeremy's light go off and Rose's go on, I knew it was finally time to move. I had been waiting in my car for them to finish their little father daughter talk. I'm sure that he told her that he broke things off with me, but that was going to change very soon.

Once I made my way inside, breaking in the same way as I had the last time, I silently snuck up the stairs and headed straight for Rose's door. I could hear her on the phone talking to someone, so I waited. I didn't want anyone to know something was wrong once I entered her room. Maybe I should have waited until Jeremy left for work tomorrow morning to confront Rose. I didn't want her to scream or put up a fight and wake him.

With my head on straight and a better plan in place, I started to make my way back down the stairs. Unfortunately, right then is when Rose's bedroom door opened. Fuck...I was so busted, and I didn't have a clue as to how I was going to explain myself.

* * * * *

(Rose)

The moment I opened my door I regretted it. I had just got off the phone with Jillian and thought that I had heard my dad coming up the stairs, but after listening a little more, I couldn't quite make out the noises I was hearing. What I found was a complete shock.

I stood there face-to-face with Meredith, not Dad. I was literally frozen with terror. I couldn't move, which really sucked, because all my instincts screamed at me to run. What made it worse, was that when she looked at me, I swore I saw her eyes flash red.

"Don't panic," she whispered.

"Are you fucking kidding me? You break into my house and you're going to go with, 'don't panic'? You're crazy!" I started to race back into my room and prepared to scream, but then I didn't have any idea what this demon bitch was capable of and I didn't want to risk her hurting my dad. She caught me by the elbow just as I reached the doorjamb.

"We need to talk. Let's go downstairs so we don't wake Jeremy." She nodded her head towards the stairs as she tightened her grip on my arm.

"Fine. But one wrong move and I'm screaming my head

off." I jerked my arm out of her grasp and pushed past her to make my way down the stairs. She was a demon, but she didn't know that I was onto her just yet. And there was no way that I was giving her the satisfaction of scaring me in my own home.

Once we reached my dad's study, I ushered her in and shut the door behind us. "What the fuck are you doing in my house in the middle of the night? I should call the cops right now you crazy bitch." I wasn't sure how long I could keep the tough girl act up, but I hoped she would buy it long enough for me to dial Christian on my cell phone.

"I would watch your mouth if I was you, little girl." She took a step towards me, just as I hit send. "You have no idea who you're dealing with or what I'm capable of."

We continued to circle each other as I watched her eyes take on the red tint again. "Who are you? And why are you so interested in my dad?" I was hoping that I could trap her into revealing that she was in fact the demon while Christian was listening on the phone. And it worked.

"From the look on your face and from the company that you keep, I think you know exactly who I am. Or should I say...*what* I am." She must have felt like she had the upper hand because she calmly sat down behind my dad's desk. "I'm a demon Rose; the very one in fact that infected your friend and killed your mother."

* * * * *

(Christian)

It was barely 8 p.m. when my cell phone vibrated in my pocket. It was Rose's number. I smiled as I made my way to somewhere quiet so that we could talk. I hoped that everything had gone alright with her father.

The moment that I clicked send, I heard Rose's voice.

"Who are you and why are you so interested in my dad?"

Fuck, something was wrong. I obviously knew she was confronting Meredith, but I had no idea where they were.

The next thing I heard was Meredith's voice. "From the look on your face and from the company that you keep, I think you know exactly who I am. Or should I say...*what* I am. I'm a demon Rose; the very one in fact that infected your friend and killed your mother."

Double fuck. This was not good, but apparently my psychic ability paid off again. By having Rose return home, we now knew exactly who the demon was. Rose had been right, and now it sounded like she might just end up paying for it with her life.

I listened to the "whoosh" of air leave Rose's lungs. She must have fallen onto the floor in shock from Meredith's confession. "Why? Why did you kill my mom? And, is that why you're here? Did you break into my house again so you could kill me, too?"

Good girl Rose. In a flash I was racing towards her house. With my preternatural vampire speed, I would be there in minutes. *Hang in there, baby.*

Once I arrived at Rose's house, the only two lights on were the one upstairs and the other down. It only took a moment for me to focus my hearing and pinpoint Rose and Meredith's voices coming from the back part of the main floor.

I raced around the back of the house and found the backdoor open. This must have been where Meredith had broken in. I silently made my way towards the room that contained the love of my life and the demon who was threatening her.

As I started to open the door, I heard Meredith say, "You *will* help me win back your father, or I'll tell him that you and your vampire friends were responsible for your mother's death."

How did she think that would work? I'm sure Mr. Reynolds would believe his daughter over his girlfriend. And talking about vampires would only cause him to think she was crazy. But then she continued.

"Don't you remember that I can control a vampire once they bite me? All I would have to do is have another vampire bite me and then force them to reveal themselves to your dad. He would have no choice but to believe me if he came face to face with a vampire, now would he?"

Damn, I guess she had a point. How in the hell was I supposed to protect Rose when I couldn't bite Meredith without becoming infected. I knew nothing about how to defend against a demon. Oh well...I guess it was time to learn.

The moment I opened the door and flew to Rose's side, Meredith's eyes began to glow red. "How dare you interfere? This has nothing to do with your kind."

"You involved my kind the second you infected Terrance, you bitch. And there is no way in hell that I'm letting you hurt Rose. I may not be able to bite you in order to kill you, but I can certainly rip you limb-from-limb. And trust me, now that we know your kind exists, my clan will make sure we destroy every single one of you. You're never going to use us or hurt anyone we love again."

As I watched the red light radiate from Meredith's eyes, I considered just grabbing Rose and speeding away from the house. But since we had no idea why she was so interested in Rose's dad, I just couldn't leave him alone without knowing if she would kill him.

"I may not be as strong as you, but after I killed Rose's mom I became a lot stronger than your average human. I'm sure it came from drinking in her essence like my ancestors used to do, and now...I think you'll find me a lot harder to kill." It sounded like she wasn't sure of her abilities, but she certainly wasn't backing down either.

She launched herself across the room, grabbed Rose, and flew out the door. Damn, she definitely had some speed. I raced after her and caught up with them in the living room, but to my surprise, she wasn't hurting Rose, but instead was whispering something in her ear that left Rose completely limp with shock. I didn't have time to wonder what they were discussing because I was too worried that any moment Meredith would snap Rose's neck.

I sped around and grabbed Meredith from behind I was able to restrain her, but it was taking quite a bit of effort. "Rose, grab the poker from the fireplace. You're going to have to kill her. And hurry, I can't hold her for much longer."

* * * * *

(Meredith)

The moment that Rose's vampire arrived, an idea formed in my head. I knew that I wasn't going to be able to beat him in a fight or outrace him if I tried to run, so instead I thought that I would take this opportunity to set both of them up.

I heard Jeremy start to stir upstairs, so I knew it would only be a matter of time before he came to find us all. So the moment I saw the opportunity, I grabbed Rose and sped towards the living room.

I hadn't lied to Christian. When I had drunk Loraine's blood, it definitely had an effect on me. I was so euphoric when I felt her essence flow into me, but what I failed to share was that in addition to the euphoric feeling, it had also infused me with her actual life force.

After I killed her, I had traveled to my grandmother's house to ask her about the old ways. She'd informed me that the demons of old drank human blood to not only absorb their essence, but because it actually lengthened their lifespan. Through the drinking of blood, the ancient demons had gained strength, speed, and the ability to defy death. Drinking human blood had started to make them immortal. But the transformation hadn't been completed and when they were faced with the extinction of their race, the old ways were lost. We had never consumed human blood because it was uncertain how it would affect us.

I had been the first to risk it, and now it looked like I was going to be putting the rest of the myth to the test as well. I had hoped that by drinking Loraine's blood I would start to become immortal or at least a little less destructible so when Rose "killed" me, I wouldn't really be dead. I didn't see any other way as Christian had already threatened to hunt me down from this point forward. So, honestly, what did I have to lose?

Once I had gotten Rose alone in the living room, I knew I only had a couple of seconds before Christian was going to be on us again. I may have gained in speed and strength, but I would never be as fast as a vampire.

"Rose, you wanted to know why I was so interested in your dad? It's because he's a demon too. And so are you." I felt her go limp with shock, just as Christian entered the room. "If Christian finds out, his clan will kill you both."

Christian sped around behind me and held me in place as he instructed Rose to do exactly what I wanted her to do.

Jeremy was rounding the bottom of the stairs just as Rose followed Christian's directions and grabbed the fireplace poker.

She ran back around and positioned herself in front of me, and with a rage-filled look on her face, she took aim.

* * * * *

(Rose)

I couldn't believe what Meredith had just whispered in my ear. Me and my dad were demons too? That was why she had been interested in my dad and killed my mom.

Just as I had started to scream at her in denial, Christian raced into the room and grabbed Meredith from behind. "Rose, grab the poker from the fireplace. You're going to have to kill her. And hurry, I can't hold her for much longer," I heard him say.

I could barely process what he was saying, but the malicious smile that spread across her face was enough to propel me into motion.

I was so angry that I could almost feel the heat radiating from my face. "I don't care if you're lying or not, I will not let you hurt my family anymore."

I had never thought that I would be capable of actually killing someone, but the moment that Meredith had confessed that she was the one who killed my mother all I could think about was her demise.

I slammed the poker into her stomach and watched her collapse into a bloody heap on the floor. That was when I heard my father scream.

CHAPTER FORTY-THREE

Clean Break

(Meredith)

I met Jeremy's eyes just as his daughter rammed the poker through my stomach. His eyes went wide with shock and he screamed.

I collapsed into a heap on the floor and laid as motionless as possible. The stab wound definitely hurt and I'm sure it looked fatal to everyone in the room, but I could already tell that it was starting to mend itself. I guess the theory of my demon immortality was proving true. I laid there listening to my plan fall into place as Jeremy started screaming at his daughter.

I knew she wouldn't try to explain that I was a demon, and

that Christian was a vampire. So my secret was safe until I decided to share it with Jeremy. So right now it just looked like his precious Rose was guilty of attempted murder. *Perfect!*

"What have you done? My God Rose, what have you done? You've killed her!" Jeremy kept repeating his panicked questions as he made his way over to me.

"I...I'm sorry. I...Dad, she killed Mom." Rose had no way to prove it, so I hoped that Jeremy would blow it off as an excuse of a desperate girl who had just tried to kill her dad's girlfriend.

"I don't understand! Tell me what happened. Please, honey, tell me exactly what happened!" He was screaming by the time he knelt down next to my body.

* * * * *

(Rose)

I had no idea what to say to my dad. There was no way to explain that Meredith was a demon, and that Dad and I were, too.

I saw Christian watching me while my dad approached Meredith. I think he was trying to remain out of the way in case he needed to react in a hurry. I'm sure he was just waiting to see what I was going to do before he spoke up. I wasn't sure what was going to happen next, but looking at Christian an idea suddenly formed in my head. Since I was planning on becoming a vampire soon, this seemed like the perfect opportunity to make a clean break from my old life.

I hated the idea of leaving Dad with this image of me, but since there was no way to explain what had truly happened here,

I decided that I didn't have much of a choice.

"Dad, I promise that what I did was for the best. For you, for me, and whether you believe me or not, for Mom. I hope you don't call the cops on me, but I'll understand if you feel you have to."

I saw Christian shaking his head at me trying to get my attention. When I looked at him, he licked his fangs and motioned to my dad. *Oh my god, he was going to bite my dad and use his sedative.* I couldn't let that happen. According to Meredith my dad was a demon and would infect Christian if he bit him. *How the hell was I supposed to get out of this?* My eyes widened and I shook my head "no" at Christian. I'd have to explain myself to him later, but I was thankful that he was letting me take the lead on this.

Resolved to the fact that running was my best option, I moved to hug my dad. He was still kneeling next to Meredith, shocked into silence with a panicked look on his face. I leaned down and hugged him tight. "I love you, Dad. Please don't ever forget that."

I couldn't stand to stay and hear his response. I knew he'd plead with me to stay and that we would figure everything out, but I'd made up my mind. It was time to start my life with Christian. I looked at him and nodded my head towards the front door. In an instant we were running for his car, and we peeled out as soon as we were both inside. By the time we hit the end of the block, the ambulance was already blaring down the street towards my house.

I buried my head in my hands and began to cry. I knew Christian probably thought that it was because I was leaving my father with the impression that his daughter was a murderer, but in reality, it was because deep down, I knew that Meredith was right. I was a demon, and if Christian found out, he and his clan would want to kill me.

My life was over.

* * * * *

(Meredith)

As I laid there listening to Rose break Jeremy's heart, I knew that my plan had worked. Jeremy had seen his sweet, precious daughter "kill" me, and now she and her boyfriend were on the run. I knew that Evangeline would hide them so I'd have to convince him not to press charges and just try to let her go. I already had an idea of how to do that, and if I was right it would guarantee my spot back in Jeremy's life.

I wasn't sure when or if I would reveal our shared heritage to him, but I knew that my life was about to begin with the man I loved. Today had been a good day to die.

(Jeremy/Dad)

As I knelt next to Meredith, I couldn't help but feel all the emotions I had once felt for her surging back to the surface. When I had heard voices downstairs, I first thought that Rose had invited her boyfriend over to pick up his car, but then I had heard Meredith's voice, and the sounds of violence.

As I raced around the corner, I took in the scene before me. Rose's boyfriend had Meredith by the arms, holding her in place while Rose stood ready to stab her with a poker.

I had screamed, and then watched in horror as my daughter pierced my ex-girlfriend through the stomach. Meredith had collapsed to the ground, blood gushing from her wound.

I raced to Meredith as I tried to process how my little girl could have done something so heinous, so criminal.

"I...I'm sorry. I...Dad, she killed Mom."

I was so shocked I felt like I couldn't function. "I don't understand! Tell me what happened. Please, honey, tell me exactly what happened!" I screamed.

What she said next will haunt me until my dying days. "Dad, I promise that what I did was for the best. For you, for me, and whether you believe me or not, for Mom. I hope you don't call the cops on me, but I'll understand if you feel you have to."

I sat there completely stunned. I realized that I was truly in shock and that was why I couldn't get my brain to work. I wanted to cry out and grab her as she hugged me, but instead I felt rooted in place. In the next instant she was gone. My little girl was gone.

Suddenly, I heard a breath escape from Meredith and that kicked my brain back into gear. I jumped up and dialed 911 and then immediately returned to her side. All my attention was focused on her as she slowly opened her eyes. *Thank God she wasn't dead.* I tried keeping her still as she started to say something. I couldn't quite make it out so I lowered my head, straining to hear what she was whispering. "Don't report Rose. Protect her."

I couldn't believe what I was hearing. Here was this woman bleeding to death in my home and she wanted to protect my daughter...the person who had just tried to kill her. How did I ever think that leaving her had been the right thing to do?

Before the EMTs made their way inside, I grabbed the fireplace poker and wiped it clean, then placed Meredith's hand on the handle. I had made sure to meet Meredith's eyes as I nodded and mouthed, "Thank you."

After stabilizing Meredith's vitals, the EMTs stopped the bleeding and bandaged her wound. While loading her into the ambulance they had said the wound wasn't as bad as it looked. I climbed into the ambulance with Meredith and we headed to the hospital.

When I grabbed her hand her slight smile and the gleam in

her eyes radiated love. I couldn't believe that I had almost ruined this relationship.

"I'm so sorry." I hoped that she understood that I was apologizing for everything: for keeping her a secret from Rose in the first place, for me breaking up with her, and most of all, for my daughter just attempting to kill her. I would gladly spend an eternity making it up to her if she'd let me.

"It's okay," she whispered. "I love you. It will all be okay."

Once we arrived at the hospital, the nurses started an IV and the cops arrived to begin their questioning. I made sure that I was close enough to Meredith so that she could hear my responses. I figured that if we were all going to get out of this we'd better have our stories straight.

With Meredith listening, I lied and told them that we were having dinner and decided to follow it up with some dessert in front of the fireplace. We had started to move some of the fireplace equipment out of the way so that we could make ourselves more comfortable on the floor, and that's when Meredith tripped and impaled herself on the poker.

My God, what was I doing? I hope this worked, because if it didn't, not only would my daughter go to jail for attempted murder, but I would be right behind her for conspiracy. I couldn't believe this was happening. One wrong move and my life was over.

After running Meredith's fingerprints to verify my story, the cops ruled it an accident and thanked us for our time.

By that time Meredith had started to drop into unconsciousness from the pain medication in her IV drip. Before she fell asleep, I quickly leaned in and whispered, "I love you, too."

As I settled in the chair of Meredith's hospital room, I tried to come up with a plan to go after Rose. Now that I knew she was still seeing Christian, obviously that was where I needed to start. It stung to know that Rose had kept seeing him behind my back. If I hadn't been so crazed with keeping her safe I might actually know more about this guy, like where he lived or who he really was. But instead, I knew nothing about the boy who just stole my daughter from me.

That was something that I was going to change very soon.

CHAPTER FORTY-FOUR

Our New Life

(Rose)

By the time we reached The Rising Pit, my eyes were dry. I literally couldn't cry anymore. Just a few hours ago, everything had been so perfect. My dad had broken up with that demon bitch, I had finally gained back my freedom, and we were going to go buy me a new car the following day.

But in a flash, everything had changed. I found out that my mom had been murdered by a demon who was after my father because apparently he was a demon, too. And not only was I a demon as well, but now...I was also a murderer.

I hadn't thought twice about killing Meredith when

Christian told me to do it. Not only had I wanted revenge for my mother, but also I had to keep her from telling Christian that I was a demon.

I had no idea how I knew it, but when Meredith had admitted to killing my mother, I had felt the rage inside of me rise to the point that something physically had changed within me. It was like I had almost felt my DNA shifting. So when she told me that my father and I were demons, I knew that she was telling the truth. I also knew she was telling the truth about Christian's clan wanting to kill me if they found out I was a demon.

I had no idea how I was going to keep this secret, but then again, I had always been able to keep my thoughts hidden. *My God, that was it!* After learning about the effects of Meredith's blood on Terrance and how it kept his thoughts protected and *fuzzy*, it all made sense. No wonder I never had a problem hiding my thoughts from Evie...it was because of my demon blood.

"Rose? Are you going to be okay?" Christian's question startled me out of my inner turmoil. With everything racing around in my head, all I could do was nod in response.

"I know that what happened is something that is going to take some time to process. But you have to realize that you didn't have a choice. She killed your mom and could have hurt you or your dad. She infected Terrance and there was no way I could let her threaten anyone else in my family. Killing her was the right thing to do."

He shifted in his seat and took both of my hands in his. "We need to get you inside and tell Evie everything that happened, but first I need to ask you a question. You know that you can no longer go back to your old life, right? I'm sorry, but I won't let you be placed in a situation where you could be taken from me. I love you and I *never* want to live without you." He swallowed hard and cupped my cheek in his palm. "I will soon become the new Sire, and when I am I want you to be my consort. If you agree, I'm sure Evie will let you stay here with us from now on. We can start our new life together right away."

Oh my God. This was what I had been dreaming of for so long, but how was this going to work? I was a demon and Christian wanted me to become his consort. It was going to kill me to have to tell him that I couldn't become a vampire anymore. That I could never be his consort.

I was so scared and I knew that I would never be able to go home again. Staying with the clan seemed like the best way to stay protected. They could bite and use their sedative on anyone that came looking for me. It was the obvious choice, even if it wasn't for the same reasons as Christian thought. "Yes. I would love to stay with you and the clan. Thank you, Christian. You are truly saving my life."

"You are my life Rose, and I'll gladly spend an eternity proving that to you." He leaned over and kissed me. It was soft, tender, and filled with emotion.

The pain in my heart left me feeling like I was the one with a poker through my chest. How could I live with the man I loved while planning to lie to him every single day?

I guess I was about to learn *exactly* how to break a vampire's heart...

Coming Soon...

Look for the next novel in The Rose Trilogy:

Blood of a Red Rose

by

Tish Thawer

Available in May 2012

CPSIA information can be obtained at www.ICGtesting.com
Printed in the USA
LVOW121506080212

267761LV00002B/44/P